She turned her head aside, her shame and humiliation complete, but he took her head in his hands and gently turned it back. "We're not going through this reluctance to cooperate again, are we?" he murmured. "Lick it off. Take my finger into your mouth. Now."

Tentatively, unsure of what to expect, she allowed him to slip his finger into her mouth. The sample tasted unusual—slightly salty, she realized—but not unpleasant. She sucked until it was gone, then continued with little baby sucks until he withdrew his finger.

"Now for the real thing." he said...

Other books by

LUSCIDIA WALLACE

Katy's Awakening

THE ICE MAIDEN

LUSCIDIA WALLACE

MASQUERADE BOOKS, INC.
801 SECOND AVENUE
NEW YORK, N.Y. 10017

First Masquerade Edition 1992

First printing January 1992

ISBN 1-56333-001-6

Cover photo © 1992 Robert Chouraqui
Cover Design by Eduardo Andino

Manufactured in the United States of America
Published by Masquerade Books, Inc.
801 Second Avenue
New York, N.Y. 10017

ONE

It was one of those glittering functions, a gathering to which the elite of society had been invited. The finest champagne flowed like water, and the cream of Boston's rich and famous made sure the press was anonymously apprised of just how many zeros were on the checks that were written to whichever charity the event was to benefit.

Edward Canton stared across the room, his gaze never leaving the hauntingly beautiful Rebecca Esterbrook. For a year, from the first time he met her at a similar function, he had been obsessed with her. To his frustration she had rebuffed every attempt he made to get close to her—refused his dinner invitations, rejected his deliveries of flowers, shunned his phone calls. She had been very blunt about the fact that she found his background totally unsuitable.

He had changed his name fifteen years earlier when he was well on his way to his first million. Being a first generation American of nondescript, immigrant parents did not project the image he so desperately wanted to cultivate. Changing his name to Canton hadn't, however, helped him in his pursuit of the beauteous Rebecca.

Rebecca's background was the type that would give him the final bit of respectability he wanted, even if only by association. Her family had been prominent in Boston society since the days of the Revolutionary War and even claimed to have come over on the Mayflower. Besides, he was not accustomed to losing when he wanted something, and he wanted Rebecca Esterbrook.

He had thoroughly investigated her family's financial status. They had quietly divested themselves of almost all their holdings and were living on the last of what remained of the family fortune—putting up a facade for the world to see. And Rebecca was the worst, maintaining all the trappings of her family's social position without regard for the emotional or financial toll.

She had attended all the proper schools, moved in all the proper circles and dated only men from the most socially acceptable families. He knew her real age was twenty-seven even though she purported to be only twenty-three. He also knew what few others knew—that she had been married for three months at the age of eighteen, the marriage and subsequent divorce cloaked in secrecy. No secret stayed hidden from him for long. She had been two months pregnant when she married. The not-very-happy couple was shipped out of town to avoid scandal. Following her miscarriage they returned to Boston and were soon divorced.

Edward had silently dubbed her "The Ice Maiden." She stood almost six feet tall in high heels with her pale blond hair swept high up on her head. Her blue eyes and porcelain-like skin contributed to the aura she projected—a cold, aloof manner that could freeze the blood in a man's veins.

It was not that he needed her physical attentions. Edward had no trouble attracting female companionship. His prowess and stamina between the sheets was legendary. He was the envy of most men and the object of desire for most women. It was common knowledge that at the age of thirty-eight he was one of the wealthiest men in the country with many international holdings and a shadowy and mysterious side that hinted of something sinister.

The phrase "tall, dark and handsome" had been invented with Edward Canton in mind. He topped six feet by several inches and had a lean, athletic body. His dark brown hair was perfectly styled but looked good even when windblown or tousled. His piercing eyes constantly changed color from silver to a dark charcoal depending on his mood.

Yes, Rebecca Esterbrook was everything he coveted and lusted after. Perfect background, perfect face and perfect body. That body—he felt the heat surge through his belly and his cock twitch every time he looked at her. He quickly drained the last of the champagne from his glass, set it on a table and made his way across the room.

"Good evening, Rebecca. It's so nice to see you again." He smiled warmly as he extended his hand. Her unemotional blue eyes appraised him as she accepted his handshake in a disinterested manner. "May I get you a glass of champagne?"

"No, thank you." Her voice was as cold as her handshake, containing not a hint of warmth or passion. "If you'll excuse me…"

He watched as she turned and walked away from him. The sequined evening gown hugged her enticingly delectable curves, and her hips swayed gently as she disappeared through the crowd. He seethed inside. Once again, with a flick of an eyelash, she had dismissed him as inferior, not worth even a moment of his time. He had to restrain himself to keep from grabbing his cock and vigorously stroking away the tightness he felt in his balls.

Edward searched through the crowd of guests. His gaze landed on Katherine Treadway. She was the opposite of Rebecca—a sultry brunette who was always hot and ready. He gave her a silent signal indicating the pool house across the yard. He had to sink his rapidly hardening cock into something—or better yet, someone.

As soon as he stepped into the darkened pool house he felt Katherine's hands slip up under his jacket. Her sensual voice purred in his ear, "I was hoping you'd be here tonight. This party needs a little excitement."

He lowered the zipper down the back of her long gown and watched as it slipped off her shoulders and fell to the floor. The sight that greeted him was exactly what he expected; she wore absolutely nothing under the dress. His gaze traveled from her ample breasts with the already hardened, dark nipples to her neatly trimmed bush of brown pussy hair.

She immediately sank to her knees, unfastened his trousers and lowered them along with his briefs. Upon obtaining its freedom, his hard cock sprang to attention. It was no secret that Katherine dearly loved the taste and feel of the male organ sliding in and out of her mouth and had turned the activity into a fine art.

She sensually ran her tongue over her glossy, red lips until they were wet and shiny. Her touch elicited a quick intake of breath from Edward as she cradled his balls in her hand. With her fingers wrapped around the base of his very impressive shaft, she flicked the tip of her tongue across the end of his cock. Then she swabbed the entire head before skimming along the underside of the rigid pole.

Edward closed his eyes and placed his hands at the back of her head as she took him into her mouth. What started as gentle and sensuous sucking quickly escalated into an urgency. Katherine's moans of pleasure spurred his actions; his hips thrust forward forcing his organ fully into her mouth and down her throat. He didn't want prolonged enjoyment, he wanted quick relief. His thrusts accelerated until he pumped into her mouth with a demanding intensity.

Katherine continued to cradle his balls as she allowed him to fuck her mouth. When he hesitated for a moment, allowing the exquisite sensations to diminish just enough for him to prolong his pleasure, she pulled back and lashed the head of his cock with her tongue. She swirled around the ridge at the base of the cap, then descended along the shaft until she captured one of his balls between her teeth. She tugged gently, sucking the hot plum as far as she could into her mouth before releasing it with a wet *pop*.

Edward returned his hands to her head and drove his throbbing rod down her throat once again, suddenly intent on reaching his climax. He thrust his hips forward and back, revelling in the way Katherine's throat muscles expertly tickled him.

"Yeah, that's it. You like that, don't you?" he murmured. "You like having my big cock in your mouth. You like swallowing my sperm. I want you to take it all down your throat."

Katherine, unable to respond, simply moaned her assent as she continued to suck his cock. Her head bobbed to and fro as she let Edward use her mouth and throat the way she would have allowed him to use her hungry cunt had he so desired.

Edward growled low, losing the cultured speech patterns and modulation he had worked so hard to establish while trying to disassociate himself from his street background. "Oh, fuck. Here it comes." His cock pulsed as he held her head against his crotch and shot his hot cream into her hungry mouth.

Katherine purred softly as she swallowed every drop of his salty sperm and licked him clean. He didn't pull back from her; he wasn't finished yet. He continued to thrust his cock in her mouth as she continued to suck. In a matter of only a few moments he was once again hard and ready.

In one swift motion Edward shoved Katherine on her back in the middle of the floor, dropped between her spread legs and rammed his throbbing meatpole deep inside her ready opening. His voice was raspy, his breathing labored. "A hungry mouth followed by a hot, wet cunt—definitely your finest assets, my dear." Foregoing any other sensations, pleasures, or conversation, he plunged in and out of her hot pussy. He liked nothing better than to rear back until his cock hovered at the entrance to her tight pussy, then drive forward so that his pubic bone smacked against her moss-covered mound and his balls slapped her upturned buttocks. She was his, completely in his power. He held her arms above her head, enjoying her moans and whimpers of submission. But of course Katherine was a willing participant; she raised her hips eagerly to meet his downward thrusts and ensure that his enormous tool was completely buried in her tunnel.

Edward continued to shuttle in and out of Katherine's box, varying the length and intensity of his strokes, sometimes rotating his hips so as to stretch her sensitive membranes even more. He could feel his cock expanding as her pussy gripped it; the head already felt twice its normal size. He released her arms and moved his hands to her jiggling breasts, rolling the engorged nipples between his fingers until Katherine's cries of pleasure became mixed with gasps of pain. He lowered his lips to her tits and worried the rigid peaks the way a dog would a bone. He could feel the pebbly flesh stiffen even more between his teeth.

His sperm was boiling and threatening to erupt. With a harsh grunt he raised himself up and rammed his cock into Katherine's pussy as hard as he could. After the second stroke he could no longer restrain himself and allowed his hot cream to jet into her waiting cavern. His legs shook as the spasms raced through him. He withdrew and moved up to her mouth where her excited tongue immediately licked him clean.

Without a word to her, Edward rose, dressed, adjusted his clothes and gave his appearance a quick check in the mirror. He then returned to the party, leaving her to fend for herself.

All his encounters with Katherine had been like that. No kiss, no caress, no tender touch, no concern for her pleasure—only a fast fuck. She was the ultimate in convenience for him. A mere glance and a raised eyebrow and she was there, providing him what he wanted.

She had blown him or fucked him in dark~ned

doorways, phone booths, restaurants, empty hall-
ways, guest bathrooms at various social functions—
the greater the risk of being discovered, the hotter
and more eager she became. Once he had even come
up behind her, raised her skirt to her waist and
slipped his prick inside her while she talked on the
phone to her husband.

She was unique in that she would have one continual orgasm from the moment her tongue touched
his cock or his cock pushed past her pussy lips;
something about their body chemistry instantly
meshed.

Katherine was not the only one. There wasn't a
woman under the age of fifty who attended the various charity functions and social events who hadn't
experienced the ecstasy of his expert lovemaking
and the thrill of his love tool at least once...except
for Rebecca Esterbrook. She was his obsession. She
seemed unattainable.

He quickly scanned the crowd for a glimpse of
Rebecca, finally spotting her by the buffet table
talking to Randall Carpenter—the youngest son of
the prestigious Carpenters. She displayed the same
aloof attitude as when he had tried to talk to her.
He continued to study her.

Was she always so cold? It was more than merely
being poised and in control. Was she this cold and
unemotional in bed, too? If so, then she would turn
out to be quite a disappointment when he finally
nailed her.

In the back of his mind a bizarre thought was
forming, the kernel of an idea that needed to be
nurtured until it grew into a full-blown plan. It
would be tricky and potentially dangerous. It could
blow up in his face, causing him more trouble than
he could buy his way out of. But if it worked...He

decided it was worth the risk. First he would give her one more opportunity to be civil.

He watched as Randall Carpenter excused himself and moved on to another group of people, leaving Rebecca momentarily alone. As Randall passed him the two of them exchanged a brief but knowing look. Edward quickly moved to her side, speaking in his warmest and most charming manner. "Are you enjoying the gathering? It seems to be another successful fund raiser."

She turned and seemed to regard him as an object of mild curiosity, someone with no connection to her exalted life. "Yes, I believe they've exceeded their goal for contributions." She looked across the room as if searching for something or someone. "Well, if you'll…"

"Rebecca," he spoke quickly before she could excuse herself and leave, "I would be very honored if you would consent to share a late supper with me this evening. I have something I'd like to discuss with you, a business proposal of sorts."

She arched an eyebrow as her cool gaze drifted over him. His grooming was impeccable, his clothes custom tailored and a perfect fit, his outward manners and voice cultured and charming, his overall appearance very attractive. In fact, it was more than attractive—it was disconcerting. What was it about him that she found so disturbing and distasteful?

She frowned. He had no pedigree; he was from the wrong side of the tracks with no social standing or history. True, he was very wealthy and very handsome, but anyone could have money and good looks. Then, too, there were those persistent rumors about his shady business dealings and shadowy international connections. He frightened her.

What she refused to admit, even to herself, was

the nervousness she felt each time she experienced the magnetic pull of his sex appeal. It was an ominous type of excitement from some deeply hidden place. Sex was of no interest to her; she would not even acknowledge the possibility.

"A business proposal? Business is best discussed in a business office. Perhaps if you called my secretary and arranged a business appointment."

She saw something dark and malevolent flicker through his alert, silver eyes then quickly disappear. His voice held no hint of anything out of the ordinary. "Yes, perhaps you're right. I'll call your secretary first thing in the morning and set up an appointment. I would still be honored if you would consent to share supper with me this evening."

"I have a previous commitment for this evening." Without so much as a "thanks for the invitation" she abruptly turned and walked away from him. He watched her retreating form, his jaw set in a hard line. His decision was made; he would proceed with his plan.

Edward sat behind the large oak desk in his spacious office absentmindedly tapping a pencil against a pad of paper. He had just scheduled his appointment through Rebecca's secretary. Rebecca was to be at his office at ten o'clock the next morning. If the first part of the plan worked as it should, then he wouldn't need to resort to the next part; but, just in case...

He opened a desk drawer, removed a private phone and quickly dialed an international number. He waited a moment while the call went through, then spoke into the receiver with an air of absolute authority. "I have a very special assignment for you. Prepare the compound on the island for a lengthy stay. There will be the two of you and one guest who will occupy the special suite in the east wing. I will join you from time to time. Plan on as much as two months. I'm not sure about the departure date. Stand by for instructions."

He clicked the cradle to get a dial tone and placed another call. "Have the jet ready. I'll be heading for the island in the next few days, along with one passenger. I'll let you know about a departure date after tomorrow morning." He returned the phone to its resting place and locked the drawer.

Edward stared at the desk in deep concentration for a few more minutes, turning his decisions and the methods of carrying them out over in his mind. One way or another he would have Rebecca Esterbrook as his lover, ready and willing to fulfill his every desire, eager to make all his fantasies come true. The arrangement could be handled easily with considerable financial gain for her and her family, if she would only be reasonable.

In the back of his mind he knew that she wasn't likely to choose the reasonable course. A slightly sinister smile turned the corners of his mouth. A tremor of excitement danced through his loins as he pictured Rebecca's cold eyes burning with the fires of passion, her long, pale blond hair flowing in loose disarray rather than perfectly coiffed on top of her head. Yes, one way or another she would be his very soon now.

Gunthar turned to Elsa following his phone conversation. "It seems Edward has another special assignment for us. We'll be leaving soon for the island compound, just the two of us, then we'll be joined by Edward and one guest."

Elsa ran her fingertips across his cheek then through his sandy-brown hair. Even though he was thirty-four, he did not look a day over twenty-six. He stood almost six feet tall and possessed a hard body, the result of daily workouts. She saw the twinkle in his hazel eyes as he continued to tell her about the conversation. "He wants the special suite in the east wing prepared for this unknown guest. You know what that means."

She smiled lasciviously and ran the tip of her tongue across her lower lip. "Certainly, darling. I wonder who it is this time—a banker to be seduced, an international corporation head to be bribed or"—she expertly tickled her fingers across his bare chest then slipped her hand inside his jogging shorts and gave his limp organ a friendly squeeze—"some government official's wife who needs special attention, both yours and mine."

"It could be one of his business associates who's looking for something different and out of the ordinary. He probably can't get it from his wife and is afraid of being discovered, so he's seeking it out on his own."

She chuckled. "And he's not afraid of letting Edward know what this hidden desire is? Oh, he'll be allowed to indulge his fantasy as much and as often as he wishes, but it will cost him dearly."

Gunthar thrust his crotch against her hand, then reached down the front of her tank top and rolled her rapidly hardening nipple between his thumb and forefinger. He watched her face as her eyelids closed over her blue eyes. She tossed back her head, her short, auburn curls clinging to the dampness of her face and neck. Elsa, too, looked considerably younger than her thirty-one years. Like Gunthar, she was in excellent physical condition. They had just returned from jogging when the call came.

They had worked for Edward for the past ten

years. He still didn't know their exact relationship: husband and wife? lovers? friends? business associates?—they could even have been brother and sister for all he knew or cared. Their special and unique talents served him well, and he rewarded them handsomely for their services. It was a mutually beneficial arrangement.

He had met Elsa and Gunthar at a party in Paris, where they resided following a move from Austria. They had since moved to one of Edward's corporate apartments in London. Their job was to handle all of Edward's "special projects" anywhere in the world, a task they eagerly and enthusiastically carried out.

They particularly liked the assignments that took them to his private island, a lush tropical setting with all the luxuries of a first-rate resort. The island afforded them total and complete privacy—no accidental interruptions or unwanted intruders of any kind, no hassles with local law enforcement agencies. The small staff at the compound and the natives who lived on the island were completely trustworthy, Edward's most devoted employees. The assignments were not always of a sinister or underhanded nature. Sometimes there were parties, not really orgies but totally uninhibited gatherings—a reward for those employees who had provided exceptional service in unusual circumstances.

This was going to be different from any of their previous endeavors. Gunthar had picked up something in Edward's voice. He couldn't identify it but knew Edward well enough to know that something out of the ordinary was about to happen—something personally important to Edward. As a matter of good business practice, Edward was seldom present when something illegal or underhanded was happening— seduction, blackmail, bribery. Those "little chores" were left to the capable hands of Gunthar and Elsa.

He stopped his speculation about the assignment and turned his attention to Elsa's soft moans of pleasure. Her hand was wrapped around his hardened cock and both her nipples protruded sharply against her tank top. Her eyes held the look of lust that, after so many years, still excited him. No words passed between them, each knew what the other wanted and needed.

She quickly removed her top and jogging shorts. Her body was lean and taut. She, too, followed a daily routine of exercise. For her petite size—only three inches over five feet—she was deceptively strong, an asset that served her well in her dealings with Edward's "guests."

His gaze traced every line of her body—the curve of her neck, her compact breasts topped with pert, strawberry nipples, her slim waist and hips, her well-shaped legs that were surprisingly long for her petite stature and, to Gunthar's unending delight, the profusion of bright red pubic hair that flourished across her mound and between her thighs, extending all the way to her anus. Her long clit peeked enticingly through the bushy growth. His breathing quickened as he reached up and cupped the underside of each breast, lowering his head to take one of her delicious nipples into his mouth.

He thoroughly enjoyed his lovemaking with Elsa. The others were simply part of the job, she was special to him. Her appetite seemed to be as insatiable as his as far as sex—in all of its various manifestations—was concerned.

That was how they had met, twelve years ago at a party in Vienna. She was only nineteen but already well versed in the ways of the flesh. As soon as he had arrived at the party their eyes had met and their gaze had locked. He had grabbed her hand and pulled her into the nearest bedroom, and they hadn't reappeared at the party until five hours later—exhausted but happy. They had been together ever since.

Their job with Edward was exactly to their liking. Gunthar had said, on many occasions, that he would rather fuck than breathe. Elsa would show her agreement by rubbing her crotch against his body.

He released her nipple from his mouth and quickly removed his own jogging shorts. His rigid cock stood straight up, demanding some attention. Elsa, her pussy juices already flowing in anticipation, put her arms around his neck and pulled herself up, wrapping her legs around his hips. His hands cupped her bottom, and in a practiced motion, he thrust his prick past her pussy lips all the way up her love tunnel.

She quivered as he filled her. No one, not even Edward himself with his powerful tool and incredible expertise, excited her the way Gunthar did. Her pussy muscles grabbed his rigid shaft and held him in a viselike grip. She was so hot for him that she lost all control. The convulsions started immediately. She clung tightly to him, whimpering and moaning as her body shuddered through an intense orgasm.

Gunthar smiled and a hint of amusement crept into his voice. "We seem to have a hot and very hungry little cunt today. If I didn't know better, I'd say it's been too long since it's had any attention." He carried her into the bedroom still impaled on his rigid cock with her legs wrapped around his hips.

He swiftly deposited her in the middle of the bed, his lance still solidly embedded in her hot cunt. Without a wasted moment he began pumping her with long strokes that soon turned into rapid jabs.

His arms were buried underneath her, his hands squeezing her buttocks in rhythm with his stroking.

Elsa grabbed his ass and exerted additional pressure on each of his downstrokes as she pushed her hips upward against his, trying to take as much of him inside her as was possible. She loved the feel of his solid cock as it slid in and out of her, as his pubic patch meshed with hers, as each thrust tickled her long clit.

Gunthar gasped for breath as he neared the edge. He couldn't get enough of her pussy, the way her love tunnel exactly fit the curve of his hard shaft. It was as if their two parts were cast from the same mold so that they fit perfectly. He expelled one last hard breath as he rammed into her as far as he could. He squeezed her ass as he spurted his hot liquid deep inside her.

Taking but a brief moment to catch his breath, he turned around and buried his mouth in her abundant bush. His lips tugged at the long strands of her pussy fur, he lapped and sucked as his cream oozed out of her dripping slit. When he had consumed the last drop he flicked his tongue up and down the sides of her engorged clit until she writhed frantically beneath him. When her moans and erratic movements reached a level he knew very well, he took the length of her clit into his mouth and began to suck—first gently, then with more force.

Elsa's moans and cries had become almost screams by the time he took her into his mouth. He loved to tease her this way, exciting her into a frenzy before actually drawing her love button between his teeth. He knew how much she loved to have her clit sucked—if she had to give up every sex act except one, that would be the one she would choose to keep. Sometimes his mouth would propel her to so many intense orgasms, one right after the other, that she feared she would actually go mad from the intensity of the prolonged pleasure.

Gunthar's still-hard cock bobbed seductively above her mouth, bouncing lightly against her lips. She quickly took him into her mouth, relishing the combined tastes of his cream and her own love juices. In a matter of moments she pulled his entire length deep into her throat.

For the next hour they ravenously consumed each other, oblivious to anything and everything else in the world. Elsa gorged herself on Gunthar's hefty meatpole. Anxious for him to maintain his stamina and the hardness of his cock, she expertly manipulated him with her tongue and lips. She licked him up and down the length of his shaft, swirled around the head, and laved the bridge between his balls and anus. Occasionally she swallowed him whole, letting her throat muscles stimulate him until she could feel him swell prior to orgasm. Then she would release him and clasp the base of his shaft and his balls tightly until the spasm passed and he was ready to begin again. In this way she kept him primed until she was ready to pull the trigger and grant him the release he craved.

For his part, Gunthar avidly devoured Elsa's sweet pussy. He nibbled at the sensitive outer folds and washed the thick mossing of hair on her mount with his tongue until her bush glistened. He inevitably returned to her pouting slit and ministered to it eagerly, licking it and darting inside it until Elsa began to squirm beneath him.

Using his hands to separate the fleshy ridges, he lapped at the pink inner membranes and scoured as much of her tunnel as he could. Her abundant juices wet his face and dribbled down his chin; he paused only a moment to catch every drop with his tongue before returning to his task, eager to send Elsa over the precipice to ecstasy—only a moment away if the pressure of her thighs around his head was any indication.

As darkness invaded their bedroom, Gunthar stirred awake. Elsa was still asleep, his limp organ resting on her tongue with her lips closed around its base. Using the last bit of lingering daylight to see, he carefully parted the bushy growth between her open legs and inspected her precious love box.

Her outer pussy lips were still red and swollen. He wasn't surprised; he had voraciously consumed his love feast. Her inner pussy lips, like her clit, were longer than usual. Even with her thighs together, her inner lips protruded past her outer lips and were completely visible. Also like her clit, they were extremely sensitive and she loved to have him lick them.

His hot breath tickling through her thick pussy fur woke her and excited her senses. She moaned softly and, without opening her eyes, raised her head and licked his balls. Her tongue continued up the separation of his bottom and pressed against his anus. Little shivers raced through her as he gently lapped at her inner pussy lips while she returned the favor on his pouting bumhole.

Edward glanced at his watch. It was approaching ten o'clock. Rebecca would be arriving in fifteen minutes. He felt irritation at his own nervousness. He was seldom nervous or unsure—that was one of the things that made him such a tough negotiator in his business dealings, both legitimate and otherwise. He read the final draft of the contract he intended to have her sign; he wanted her as his lover, but it was still a business deal he was offering her.

"Mr. Canton, Miss Esterbrook is here."

Edward flipped the switch on the intercom. "Send her in, Emily." He rose from his chair and stood behind his desk as Rebecca made her way across the room. He silently admired the way she walked, gracefully yet with a sort of sensual undulation. She was, as always, perfectly coiffed and made up. She wore a white linen suit that somehow managed to be without a single wrinkle or crease anywhere in the fabric. Her silk blouse was the palest shade of blue. Once again the Ice Maiden projected an aura of cold restraint in both her attitude and appearance.

He extended his hand toward her and offered his most charming smile. "Good morning, Rebecca. Please," he indicated the chair across the desk from him, "have a seat. May I offer you some coffee or tea?"

She accepted his handshake in her usual cool manner, then seated herself. "No, thank you. My time is limited. Could we get right to this business matter?"

His pleasant outer manner belied the spark of anger that ignited in response to her attitude. "Certainly." He seated himself behind his desk. Without further conversation he withdrew a file folder from a drawer, reached inside it and handed her the contract form. "I believe this is self-explanatory."

He leaned back in his chair and watched as she read the document. He saw the initial confusion cross her face then the anger come into her pale blue eyes. She continued to read until she had digested every word, then placed the contract on the desk. When she looked up at him the fires of anger flashed from her eyes.

He allowed a slight smile to curl the corners of his

mouth. "That's the most emotion I've ever seen you show. I was beginning to wonder if you really *were* made of ice."

She didn't say a word as she rose from the chair and started to turn toward the door.

"One moment, Rebecca. Before you allow your sense of false pride to send you out my door," she turned back toward him and watched as he picked up the file folder he had placed on his desk—"You should know I have a complete dossier on you and your family's financial status. It's not a very pretty picture. I'm offering you quite a substantial amount of money—2.4 million dollars payable in monthly increments of two hundred thousand over the next twelve months with an option for an additional twelve months. I would think, considering your current financial condition, that you would at least give more than a passing thought to such a lucrative offer."

He saw the anger disappear from her eyes to be replaced with fear and uncertainty at the mention of her family's dire financial problems. She showed a momentary flash of confusion and vulnerability but quickly covered it with her cold aloofness. "What you are offering me, Edward, is a great deal of money to be your personal whore."

He studied her for a moment as she stared defiantly at him. "I'm sorry you've decided to reject my offer."

A slight shiver moved up her spine as the sinister glow appeared in his silver eyes. She didn't know what to make of it other than it frightened her. She had expected him to say more, to plead his case. He was right, it was a very substantial amount of money and she and her family could certainly use it. She had just witnessed a quick glimpse into how he conducted business: no give and take, no back and forth, no offer and counteroffer—just the hard reality of take it or leave it on his terms. An uneasiness settled in the pit of her stomach as she continued to silently stare at him.

He returned her unwavering look. "Unless you have something to add or want to reconsider my offer, I assume our meeting is concluded." He leaned back in his chair and looked away, waiting for her to speak.

Rebecca wasn't sure what to do. She had never encountered this type of situation before and certainly had never been exposed to this type of business proposal. He had put her on the defensive then dismissed her as if she were a nobody. Totally flustered and not knowing what else to do, she turned and left his office.

Two

"Make arrangements to leave for the island first thing in the morning. I'll fax you a file this afternoon. It will tell you all you need to know." Edward hung up the phone, quickly checked his appointment calendar, then dialed another number. "We'll leave for the island in three days, probably close to midnight—myself and one other person. Gunthar and Elsa are leaving from London tomorrow morning."

Having taken care of his final instructions he settled back in his chair. In three days Rebecca would be attending an exclusive gallery opening. He owned the limo company that would be providing the chauffeurs and cars for the invited guests. That was when he planned to take her, upon her departure from the gallery. It would be his driver who would take her directly to his company's private airstrip and his waiting jet.

For the next three days he busied himself with preparations to be away from his office for a few days. He made a last minute check with Gunthar to make sure his instructions had been received, understood and carried out prior to Rebecca's arrival on the island.

A million fears and curiosities soared through Rebecca's mind as she luxuriated in her bath. Edward had offered her, in writing, a lot of money to be his lover. It had been so cold and impersonal, the way he made it a business proposal. She had to admit that she found him intriguing. She had heard the other women gossip about his sexual prowess and, on occasion, had allowed her mind to wander in that direction. Still, though, he frightened her. There was something quite sinister and dark about him.

During the past three days she had begun to breathe easier. He hadn't called her, hadn't sent any messages, hadn't tried to contact her in any way. She was relieved that he had apparently decided to abandon his pursuit of her.

She stepped from the scented bath water and reached for a large bath towel. The limo would be picking her up in two hours and taking her to the gallery opening. She had been looking forward to this evening for several weeks now. One of the sponsors of the gallery were the Carpenters—Randall would be at the opening representing the family.

Randall Carpenter—just the type of proper social background she required and a family fortune to put her own family back on its feet. She would show Edward Canton she didn't need his money or his obscene offer to pay her for sex.

She wouldn't have to worry about sex with Randall either. While he was very good-looking and rich, he was totally ineffectual and quite boring. There were even rumors that he was gay. The family desperately wanted him to marry if for no other reason than to stop the rumors and avoid an embarrassing scandal.

That was perfectly okay with Rebecca. She could put up with the boredom. And as far as sex was concerned—well, after the horrible things she had experienced during those three months she was married, she could certainly do without sex for the rest of her life. The physical pain and the humiliation still haunted her after all these years.

She dressed and was waiting when the limo came to pick her up. Something about the way the driver looked at her, some hidden knowledge in his eyes, bothered her. He said and did nothing improper, so she dismissed the nagging worry. When they arrived at the gallery, the driver asked what time he should have the car waiting for her. She glanced at her watch and told him ten o'clock would be fine.

Once Rebecca had entered the gallery the car driver quickly dialed a number on the car phone. "It's on for ten o'clock." The driver replaced the car phone and pulled the limo away from the curb.

Edward glanced at his watch. So, just a few short hours from now. The driver would pick him up and take him to the airstrip, then return to the gallery and get Rebecca. He felt a tight tugging in his belly as he thought of the weeks ahead; a burning urgency deep inside him made his cock twitch and his pulse race. *In just three hours, Rebecca, you will be in my control for as long as I choose.*

The driver tipped his hat and held the limo door open for Rebecca as she slid gracefully into the back seat. In a matter of moments the vehicle pulled away from the curb and blended into the traffic. Four blocks down the street the driver took a left turn.

"Driver, you're going the wrong way." The only response to her words was the sound of the doors locking and the window between her and the driver closing, effectively shutting off all further communication. A sudden feeling of panic welled up inside her. She knocked on the glass separating her from the driver, but he either did not hear or simply refused to acknowledge her. The limo continued to the outskirts of town, to a private airstrip. On the tarmac, with the door open and the steps down, sat a sleek jet. The limo pulled up next to the plane.

The driver opened the door for Rebecca. "This is where you get out."

"I'll do no such thing. I demand you take me home immediately, or I'll call the authorities."

He leaned his head into the car. For the first time she got a good look at his face. It was not exactly mean or cruel, but it was hard and definitely meant business. She was sure the ugly scar on his right cheek had been the result of some sort of violence rather than an accident.

"You got two choices, lady. Either you walk or I throw you over my shoulder like a sack of potatoes and carry you. One way or the other you're getting on the plane."

Her earlier panic quickly turned into fear. There was no one around, just the two of them, her and this hulking man who looked like he was capable of any number of unpleasant things. Her heart pounded as she tried to bring her fears under control. The quaver in her voice gave her away. "Whose plane is it? Where am I going?"

Without any further conversation, he reached into the car, grabbed her arm and pulled her out. With a swiftness surprising for his size, he slung her over his shoulder and carried her up the stairs into the jet. He unceremoniously plopped her into a seat and fastened the seat belt across her lap. As he turned to leave, the pilot came out of the cockpit and followed him to the exit. As soon as the chauffeur had cleared the stairs, the pilot pulled them up and secured the door.

"I demand to know where you're taking me and who is responsible for this outrage." Her voice was as indignant as she was able to make it considering her insides were churning into knots.

The pilot barely looked at her and said, "We'll be taking off immediately." He disappeared into the cockpit and started the engines. A moment later the plane started its taxi toward the runway. In less than five minutes they were in the air and heading out over the ocean.

Tears welled in her eyes. She had not felt this frightened since that night Jason had attacked her—"date rape" was the term now used to describe her loss of virginity and subsequent pregnancy. Jason had told her, all the while pounding his dirty little prick into her, that it was all her fault. He had been dating her for two months, and she had refused to put out, like she thought she was too good for him. He said he knew she really wanted it but she was just being one of those high society bitch cock-teasers.

The humiliation that followed was almost more than she could bear. When he had finished with her he just laughed and told her she was a lousy lay. She had considered herself lucky he hadn't followed up by doing what he had threatened to do—jam his still-hard pole into her mouth and make her swallow his disgusting sperm. Then when she found she was pregnant, her parents actually paid him to marry her so the baby would be legitimate.

The following three months that she spent married to Jason had been a living hell. She'd sworn she would never have sex again for the rest of her life and, in fact, had been celibate since that time. She didn't understand how other women could talk about it as if it were some wondrous magical experience, lots of fun, the ultimate sensation. Not even for 2.4 million dollars could she voluntarily allow a man to insert his vile organ into her.

The sound of a door opening and closing behind her startled her out of her thoughts. Someone else was on the plane besides her and the pilot. She twisted around in her seat and found herself staring directly at Edward Canton. She gasped as the full magnitude of the situation settled over her.

He went directly to the bar and poured two glasses of wine, then handed one to her. "You know, Rebecca, you really should have accepted my offer. You'll find that I always get what I want. It would have been much easier all the way around. This, however," he allowed a hint of a smile to turn the corners of his mouth, "promises to be much more exciting."

She tried her best to maintain her aloof attitude. "This plane has to land somewhere and when it does I shall see to it that the authorities—"

"Oh, this plane *will* land somewhere, but I'm afraid there won't be any authorities for you to contact, no one to turn to for help, no means of communicating with the outside world without my permission and no avenue of escape. You see, where we're going I *am* the 'authorities.'"

"So you've stooped to the level of a common rapist." She tried to make her voice as contemptuous as she could.

"Rape? If I were interested in merely raping you I could have done that a long time ago. I could be doing it right now; there's nothing and no one here to stop me. You are totally and completely at my mercy."

Her fears clouded her better judgment. She threw the glass of wine at him. Almost as if she was watching it in slow motion, she saw the wine leave the glass and splash into his face. Then she saw his eyes darken as the anger crossed his countenance.

She stammered, unable to clearly define what she was trying to say. "Oh...I didn't mean...I'm..." Fear choked off her words.

Edward set down his wine glass, picked up a bar towel and wiped his face. Displaying a remarkable amount of control he spoke to her very calmly, carefully measuring his words. "We will be working with a system of rewards and punishments. When you behave in the manner required, perform with enthusiasm, exhibit newly acquired skills, there will be rewards. However, when you disobey or show bad judgment, as you just did, there will be punishments.

"The first thing we must do is make sure you understand your place and status. We are no longer in Boston society, we are in my realm. Your status is the lowest possible until you have earned the right to progress up the ladder. The privileges you claim as your birthright have no meaning where we are going. You have no rights other than those I choose to grant you."

He stood motionless in front of her, towering over her like an ominous statue that had been dredged up from the bottom of her deepest fears. She gave up all pretense of bravery, superiority and defiance. She was truly frightened. "What are you going to do with me? Please, don't hurt me, I'll do what you want."

His voice was cold, hard. "Yes, you certainly will—you'll do exactly what I want, when I want and where I want." He reached out his hand and ran his finger across her cheek and down the side of her neck. He felt her body stiffen and then tremble under his touch.

"We'll start right now. Your inexcusable behavior with the wine glass has earned you your first punishment." He deftly unhooked the seat belt, grabbed her arm and pulled her to her feet. He stared intently at her for a long moment. He saw the fear in her eyes. The Ice Maiden was no longer cold and aloof, she was truly fearful for her own safety. The situation pleased him.

He turned and started toward the door to the back cabin pulling her along behind him. He opened the door and shoved her into the room—an executive bedroom used on long flights. He released her wrist from his grasp and closed the door. She cowered in the corner, trying to make herself disappear from his sight.

Edward pulled his shirt out from his jeans and began unbuttoning it. He removed it as he watched the expression on her face. Without warning he grabbed her and pulled her body against his. One hand stayed in the middle of her back, holding her to him. His other hand twined in her perfectly coiffed hair, forcing her face to his. He captured her mouth with a burning intensity, forced his tongue between her tightly closed lips, breathed the fires of his passion into her.

She doubled up her fists and pushed against his chest, trying desperately to break his hold on her. He had moved with such suddenness that he caught her completely off guard. All she could think was that he was going to do it to her right then and there and laugh at her afterward, as Jason had done so many years ago. She pushed harder against his chest, trying to escape his clutches. She would never give in to him. He could force her compliance, but she would never willingly give herself to him.

With the same suddenness he released her and stepped back. He paused for a moment as he watched her try to recover her composure from his unexpected actions. *So, the Ice Maiden does have some fire buried inside her, whether she admits it or not.*

He casually reached in the closet for a clean shirt. A hard smile came to his mouth as he noted her fearful attention to his actions. "Relax, I'm only changing my shirt. This one has wine on it." He studied her for a moment longer. "Let me put your mind at ease, at least for the time being. It won't happen now and it won't happen here." He paused to take in her reaction to his words. He was again pleased with what he saw.

After calming her immediate worries he provided her with an even greater set of fears. "But rest assured, it will happen." He grabbed her shoulders and pulled her to him again. He removed the pins from her hair so that it cascaded to her shoulders. His voice became soft and sensual as he continued to talk to her. "Not only will it happen, it will happen again and again. It will happen in more ways than you're able to imagine and at times when you least expect it.

Day after day, even week after week or month after month if that's what it takes."

His lips nibbled seductively at the corner of her mouth, then moved across her cheek and down the side of her neck. He felt her body stiffen and tremble with fear as he held it against his. He whispered in her ear: "You'll remain my captive until you learn to be the perfect lover, until you beg me over and over again to fuck you into exhaustion, until your only desire in life is to willingly satisfy me in any and all ways, until you are able to completely fulfill my every fantasy no matter how depraved you may find it, until your every waking minute is consumed with your need for my cock."

The tears welled in her eyes as she listened to his words. This must surely be a dream, a terrible nightmare. This couldn't really be happening to her. She closed her eyes hoping that when she opened them she would be in her own house—in her own bed.

"Rebecca!" The word was an order, demanding and harsh. She immediately opened her eyes. He had put on a clean shirt and was once again neatly dressed even though his attire was casual. For a moment the image of his bare upper torso flashed through her mind. His chest and arms were muscular, like a well-conditioned athlete, his waist trim and his stomach hard and flat. His tanned skin indicated a lot of time spent in the sun.

Her attention snapped back to what he was saying, his voice still harsh. "...your punishment. Remove that evening gown. It's totally inappropriate for where we're going." She stared at the hard lines of his handsome face. She remained riveted to the spot, not moving. She made no attempt to comply with his demands.

He saw the bewilderment and confusion on her

face as she stood staring at him, seemingly not knowing what to do. He was torn between repeating his order and dramatically demonstrating to her the necessity of obedience. He chose the latter. In one swift movement he wrapped his hand around the fabric at the gown's neckline and yanked it down—literally ripping the gown from her body.

She gasped in shock and instinctively reached for the torn fabric to try and cover herself. "My gown, look what you've done to my beautiful gown."

Edward stepped back from her. His voice contained just a hint of surprise. "Where are your priorities? I've just ripped your dress from your body. At any moment I could violently rape you and your only concern is that your dress has been ruined! Are you really that shallow?" He was beginning to wonder if he had cut a bad deal for himself, whether she was going to really be worth all this trouble and expense.

He sat on the edge of the bed. "Take off the rest of your clothes, Rebecca. I want to see what I'm getting. I'm not accustomed to buying something without first inspecting the goods." His words were cold and biting, just as he had intended.

She felt the sharp sting of his words and saw the total lack of emotion in his eyes. She didn't know why she had blurted out that bit about him ruining her gown. He was right: that should have been the least of her worries. And now, he was ordering her to disrobe in front of him so he could inspect her as if she were a piece of merchandise on the auction block. She closed her eyes as the humiliation swept through her.

"Right now, Rebecca. Take them off or I'll rip them off you."

The gown had been a very pale lavender. It occurred to him that all her clothes were either white or very pale pastels—no flash, no color, no excitement. Her body visibly trembled as she removed the rest of the gown. Her bra and panties were both the same shade of pale lavender. Even her pantyhose were lavender. She removed the pantyhose, then stopped.

"Everything. I want to see you standing before me without a stitch on, as naked as the day you were born."

The tears were trembling at the brink of her eyelids and threatening to overflow. Her voice was shaky and distraught. "Please don't do this to me. Don't humiliate me like this."

"Perhaps," he rose from the bed, "a lesson in humility is what you need. It's your punishment for the wine. You've never had a problem dismissing others as inferior. It's time you found out what it's like to be on the other side."

Without waiting to see if she would comply with his latest order, he reached his finger out and traced the edge of her lace bra across the swell of her breast. He liked the feel of her skin, smooth and silky. She trembled as she tried to shrink away from him, stepping backward, away from his touch.

"Don't even think about backing away from me. You have no place to go. You are my captive. Now," he paused for a moment as he nestled his finger in the valley between her breasts, "take the rest of it off."

Rebecca remained frozen to the spot, too terrified to move. She saw the anger flash through his eyes as, without a word, he reached out and ripped the panties from her body. Her hands immediately flew to cover her exposed pubic area. A hard smile turned the corners of his mouth as he lifted the torn panties to his nose and inhaled her feminine fragrance.

Edward dropped the panties to the floor. His voice was demanding. "The rest of it, Rebecca, take it off. I want to see your tits."

She struggled with the fasteners at the back of her bra using only one hand while trying to keep her other hand in front of her vulnerable femininity. The hooks finally gave way and the bra dropped to the floor. She placed her free hand across her exposed breasts, trying to hide them.

He yanked her hands away from her body, his breath hissing between his teeth at his first sight of her nude body. Standing before him was the most perfect form he had ever seen. She was everything he had envisioned in his mind and more—much more. From the pale blond hair cascading around her shoulders to the tips of her painted toenails she was incomparably, ravishingly beautiful.

He ran his finger across her cheek, down the curve of her neck and along the crest of her shoulder. Her breasts were firm, full, rounded, uplifted and capped by delicate, rosy nipples that puckered to taut peaks as he watched—from embarrassment rather than excitement, he was sure. He wanted one of them in his mouth. He wanted to feel the pebbled texture against his tongue.

He reached out and cupped her large mounds. They perfectly fit his curved hands, her hard nipples pushing against his palms. She recoiled at his intimate touch, her entire body trembled. "Stand still!" It was an order, not a request. He wanted to take her, to fuck her into exhaustion, but he would wait. Now was the time to savor this visual treat and anticipate. He also enjoyed the nervousness, wariness and that was clearly evident on her face and in her

His inspection tour continued. Her slim w way to gently curved hips. Her stomach w smooth, her long legs sleek and tapered. He circled her. Her bottom was perfectly rounded and smooth. He ran his fingertips across the curve of her buttocks, around her hip and across the flat of her abdomen. He heard her gasp and felt her shiver.

He again faced her. The best for last. His voice was firm and commanding without being too cold. "Get on the bed, pull up your knees and spread your legs. I'm going to be spending a lot of time in your pussy; I want to be sure my cock has a nice home."

His words caused violent tremors to course through her body. He actually expected her to open her legs for him, expose her most private and intimate place to his impersonal inspection! She closed her eyes as the tears trickled down her cheeks. Her voice was a mere whisper. "I can't do what you ask. Please don't make me."

His voice was hard, his words cut through her. "I'm not asking you, I'm telling you. You will do this, Rebecca, and you will do it now. Not only will you do this, you will do so much more. You will do anything and everything I want—willingly, grate-fully, and ultimately enthusiastically without even being asked. Yes, Rebecca. You will do this. Get on the bed and spread your legs for me. Now!"

Her words were barely audible. The tears continued to stream down her cheeks. Her entire body shook violently. "I can't...I just can't..."

Edward opened a drawer, removed some lengths of velvet cord, then turned toward her. She watched his every action with frightened eyes. "I expect to have my instructions carried out immediately and without question. You will learn obedience. Don't make me beat it into you." He cupped her chin and turned her head from one side to the other as he studied her. "It would be a shame to

40

have to mark that pretty face," he allowed his fingers to trail down her neck and across the swell of her breast, "or that beautiful body." He saw the fear in her eyes.

With surprising swiftness he shoved her back onto the bed and pulled her thighs apart, quickly placing his knees between her legs to keep them open. He deftly tied her wrists together, stretched her arms above her head and tied them to the bed frame. Then he tied each of her legs just above the knee and pulled them up and apart, securing them to the bed frame.

Once again he had given her an order then immediately followed her resistance with decisive action. She would soon learn that he had no intention of debating an issue or discussing the merits of his commands. She would immediately comply with his wishes or experience his displeasure.

Rebecca pulled against her restraints, her body wracked by sobs. "Please don't do this to me. Don't tie me up like this. I'll do what you ask. Please untie me." Edward totally ignored her pleas.

Her pussy was totally exposed, vulnerable and awaiting his pleasure. Her pubic hair was as pale blond as the tresses that spread out across the pillow where her head rested. Rather than being thick and curly, it was straight and sparse, almost giving the illusion that her entire mound had been shaved clean. The sight excited him. He felt his cock stiffen and his balls tighten. Her inner pussy lips were small, flower-delicate and pink. Her clit rested under its hood. He inserted his finger into her slit then withdrew it. She felt surprisingly tight and very dry.

At the intrusion of his finger into her most private of recesses, she pulled harder against the velvet ropes, at the same time breaking out into almost uncontrollable sobs. Her eyes were tightly shut. If she couldn't see him, couldn't see the smirk on his face as he laughed at her, then perhaps the humiliation wouldn't be as overpowering. He had, thankfully, quickly removed his finger and didn't seem to be preparing to attempt intercourse with her. Hopefully he was keeping his word about not violating her at this time.

His gaze roved from her love box to her intriguing bottom. As his glance fell on her anus his eyes narrowed. There was no doubt about it, the opening had been penetrated several times.

He lightly touched his fingertip to the rosebud. Her response to his touch was immediate and startling. She screamed, a scream of frenzied terror. He quickly withdrew his hand and watched as she thrashed hysterically at her bindings. He was very confused. He had never encountered anything like this before—hysterical women, yes, but nothing like this.

Pressing her for information seemed counterproductive. He would leave this task to Elsa. Perhaps woman to woman she could discover the reason for Rebecca's hysterical fear. He made a mental note to tell Gunthar to avoid any attempts at anal intercourse until further notice.

The original plan was for him to leave the island the next day, turning Rebecca over to Elsa and Gunthar for her total indoctrination. He had intended to use Elsa in a strong, domineering role that would drive Rebecca to Gunthar for comfort, Eventually that male comfort role would become his. But he decided their purposes would be better served if Elsa could become a confidante to

Rebecca, someone to talk to and confide in, someone to keep her from feeling totally isolated and alone. He also decided he would stay on the island for a day or two, until he could see some progress.

He untied Rebecca's legs, allowing her to lower them. Her hysterics subsided and were now quiet sobs. She was finally able to speak. "Please, Edward. Not that. Anything except that. I'll gladly do whatever you want...just not that, please."

His voice was soft and soothing, unlike his words. "You're in no position to bargain. Perhaps if you had accepted my contract we could have added a provision excluding certain things, but it's too late now. There isn't an orifice, a spot, a single square inch of space anywhere on your body that will not be available to me for whatever pleases me."

She knew that would be his answer, knew that he wouldn't make any concessions. He hadn't become as rich and powerful as he was by making concessions. She wanted to die, but knew she wasn't that lucky.

Edward turned and left the cabin, closing the door behind him, and headed for the cockpit. "I want the controls, Jack." Edward strapped himself into the co-pilot's seat and put on the headset. Among his many accomplishments was a pilot's license with a jet rating. He quickly checked the instrument panel, noted their current position and checked their heading, then settled back.

He enjoyed flying; it took his mind off everything else. This time, however, it didn't quite work. The image of Rebecca's naked body danced in front of his eyes as he mentally replayed his visual inspection of her.

He couldn't erase the picture of her nipples

puckering or the sight of her delicate pussy lips. He frowned slightly as he recalled how tight and dry she felt. Could it be possible that she had very little sexual experience and none of it enjoyable? He again flashed on her hysterical reaction when he had touched her anus. He hadn't expected quite so strong a response. It was vaguely unsettling.

Edward shook his head to clear it and turned his mind back to the task at hand as the jet streaked through the night sky.

THREE

Half an hour from their destination Edward turned the controls of the jet over to the pilot and walked back to the cabin. He found Rebecca awake, her eyes red and puffy from crying and her mascara smeared under her eyes and down her cheeks.

He went to the bathroom and returned with a damp wash cloth. He carefully patted the cool water on her face and closed eyes then wiped away the smeared mascara. "There, that should make you feel better. I know it makes you look better. We'll be landing soon."

He released her arms from above her head and untied her wrists. She huddled in the corner, pulling the bedspread around her body. She took the damp cloth from him and continued to dab at her burning eyes. "Landing? Where?"

"On an island, a private compound. It's quite luxurious, with all the comforts you're accustomed to having. There's a robe in the closet. You can wear that for now. Everything you need is already in your suite."

His words left her confused. A private compound on some island with luxurious living conditions and a suite for her? More importantly, things already in place specifically for her? How long had he been planning this? Was this his real intention from the beginning, knowing she would never sign that contract?

She slowly rose to her feet, making sure the spread was wrapped fully around her body. Before she could reach the closet to fetch the robe, however, he pulled the spread away, leaving her standing naked in front of him. She visibly trembled as he looked at her.

"The spread stays on the bed, not around you."

She mustered up as much defiance as she could, at the same time trying to cover her nakedness by placing one hand in front of her mount and her arm across her breasts. She glared at him. "I don't understand why I'm being forced to stand around in the nude while you get to remain dressed." She had hoped he would respond by allowing her to cover up. Once again she had underestimated him.

He held her look as he silently began unbuttoning his shirt. He shrugged out of it, again revealing his well-toned upper torso. Her eyes widened with surprise, then her gaze involuntarily dropped from his face to his body and remained glued there as he unzipped his jeans and lowered them past his hips. He paused long enough to kick off his shoes then stepped out of the jeans and threw them aside. Next he quickly removed his socks and stood before her in just a pair of bikini briefs. His legs were long and muscular and, like the rest of his body, nicely tanned.

A teasing smile crossed his lips. "So, you want a preview—I hope this meets with your approval." Before she could blink an eye, his briefs disappeared and he stood before her in all his glory. And glory it was. She had never seen a more magnificent male body—not that she had seen that many in real life, but she had seen pictures.

She stared, mesmerized, as his cock twitched and began to grow. It was long and thick and perfectly proportioned. The head was a dark helmet that stirred before her eyes. In its flaccid state his cock was impressive, but now…She had never witnessed the transition from flaccidity to erection. It fascinated her. She had never before associated the word "penis" with the word "beautiful," but his truly was. She shivered as the magnitude of his virility washed over her.

His voice teased. "My, my, Rebecca. You're almost drooling. Do I assume that indicates approval of what you see?" He saw her head jerk up at his words, her face and eyes holding a look of shock and embarrassment. She turned her head and looked away, unable to meet his gaze.

He stepped close to her, forced his hand between her thighs and again inserted his finger between her tender pussy lips, taking a few moments to wiggle it enticingly as his thumb rubbed against her clit. He was pleased as he felt her dryness giving way to a dampness that wet his finger. "You seem to be more receptive than you were earlier. We still have ten minutes, just enough time for a quick sample of what you can expect."

Rebecca took a quick step backward, away from his touch. She took several deep, calming breaths, then she spoke in the firmest voice she could manage. "Don't confuse some sort of involuntary bodily function with anything that might possibly resemble desire on my part. Only the crudest lowlife would resort to kidnapping and rape in order to have sex. I find you loathsome."

He smiled knowingly as he backed her toward the bed, his tone of voice clearly conveying the fact that he didn't believe she meant a word of what she said. "Of course." When the back of her legs touched the edge of the bed, he rubbed his hard erection against her soft, smooth belly.

In her desperate attempt to get away from his disturbing closeness, she fell back across the bed with her legs dangling over the edge. He quickly knelt between her opened legs and again inserted his finger into her slit. He moved it slowly in and out as his thumb continued to gently stroke her clit. All the while he watched the expression on her face.

He had read her like a book. As much as she tried to project disgust and revulsion at his unwanted attentions, she knew her increased breathing gave her away. Her body that she tried desperately to control had betrayed her. She felt something, stirrings she had never before experienced. She instinctively knew that something very powerful was happening and it frightened her. She wanted the feelings to go away; she wanted Edward to go away.

"That's it, Rebecca." His voice was soft and so very sensual as he whispered the words. "Let go, enjoy. You know you want me to slide my cock past your pretty pink pussy lips, just like I'm doing with my finger. You know you want me to fill your cunt with my hardness, to fuck you like you've never been fucked before."

He ran the tip of his tongue across her lower lip as she quickly turned her head away. "You're getting so very wet, your pussy juices are starting to flow—just like a real woman, a passionate, sensual, desirous woman rather than the untouchable princess you pretend to be. Tell me, Rebecca, are you really that frigid? Have you ever experienced orgasm?"

She shuddered as his words cut through her. How could he be so perceptive about her most private and personal reality? How could he know?

He continued to slowly slip his finger in and out of her wet opening and tease her clit with his thumb. He saw and felt her reaction to his words. He had guessed right. For some reason, even though she had obviously engaged in pre-marital sex and then had been married, she had very little experience and none of it pleasurable. This whole thing was going to be much more difficult than he had originally anticipated. He would revamp the plan that night.

Now he added a new sensation. His mouth again captured hers, his tongue forcing its way between her closed lips. She tried to turn her head away, to push his hand from between her legs, but he was much too powerful for her. She could do nothing but silently endure his assault.

Edward felt the change in the plane as the pilot lowered the flaps in preparation for landing. It was time to get dressed. They would be on the ground very soon.

Without warning Edward abandoned his ministrations, abruptly rose to his feet and began dressing. He casually glanced down at her. "You'd better put on your robe unless you plan to leave the pla naked as a jaybird. We'll be on the ground in a couple of minutes." He noted the confusion in her eyes and on her face. Her cheeks were flushed and her breathing was slightly labored as she took the robe and quickly wrapped it around her. He was very pleased with himself.

She wasn't sure what had happened. As much as she hated admitting it, he had done things to her—made her feel things she had never before felt—then he had shifted gears on her as easily as if they had been engaged in nothing more than casual conversation. He had purposely titillated her body, then coldly turned away from her. She didn't know which made her angrier—her unexpected and unwanted response to his advances, or his sudden and unemotional indifference.

As she tied the sash around her waist she remembered his words...*until you beg me over and over again to fuck you into exhaustion...until your every waking minute is consumed with your need for my cock*... She shivered as his words came back to haunt her. Was it possible for his pronouncement to come true? She shivered again as she followed him from the bedroom, sat down and buckled her seat belt just moments before the jet touched down on the island runway. She closed her eyes and took a steadying breath.

Gunthar and Elsa stood next to a jeep by the edge of the runway and watched as the jet taxied off the tarmac and rolled slowly to their location. Moments later the door opened and the pilot lowered the stairs. Edward appeared in the door and quickly descended the steps. Rebecca, wearing the bright red robe with her blond hair glistening in the light of the tropical full moon, was behind him.

Gunthar let out a low whistle of appreciation. "So

that's Rebecca Esterbrook. She doesn't look so cold and aloof. Edward must have started work on the plane."

Elsa reached behind him, grabbed a handful of his ass and gave it a loving squeeze. Her voice teased, "This could be one of the best assignments we've ever had. She looks good enough to eat," she licked her lips, "literally."

They watched as Edward walked toward them, his bearing indicating to one and all exactly who was in charge. Rebecca followed, her movements and manner tentative. The confusion and fear clearly showed on her face.

He shook hands with Gunthar and gave Elsa a warm kiss and affectionate pat on the bottom before turning toward Rebecca. "This is Gunthar and Elsa. They will be with you, guiding and teaching you, until I am completely satisfied with your performance. Then, and only then, will you be allowed to return to Boston."

Without further conversation, Gunthar drove them to a large villa surrounded by a high wall. Outside the wall were several guest cottages, each one appearing to be deluxe and comfortable. Inside the wall was a sprawling house with many wings, exquisitely landscaped grounds, two tennis courts and a large swimming pool.

Rebecca was amazed. It really did look like a luxurious resort. She wondered if this was something Edward actually owned and what he used it for. Then she remembered all the whispered gossip about his shady international dealings. This was probably where he conducted that kind of business—far from prying eyes and ears.

Gunthar and Elsa disappeared as soon as they entered the house. Edward escorted Rebecca to a large suite. They entered through double doors into a spacious sitting room that was very tastefully decorated.

"This is your suite for as long as you're here. The wet bar is stocked and will be checked daily for whatever you want. There's fresh fruit and cheese in the refrigerator if you desire a snack between meals. The entertainment unit," he indicated the large cupboard against the far wall, "contains a television, VCR and CD player. I've provided a selection of classical music—that's your favorite if I'm not mistaken."

He walked across the room and opened a door. "This is a small powder room." Leaving the door open he proceeded through the sitting room to another set of double doors. "This is the bedroom and private bathroom." He opened the doors and stepped back so she could enter the room.

She stepped through the doors and came to an abrupt halt, a very audible gasp escaping her lips. She turned toward him, her eyes wide and frightened. Her voice held an edge bordering on a sob. "I can't stay in this room. Please—this is a large house, there must be another room...Don't make me stay in here."

His voice was stern but quiet. "This is your suite until I decide otherwise. There will be no discussion of the matter." He grabbed her by the elbow and steered her into the room, closing the doors behind them.

An extra-large, obviously custom-made, four-poster bed occupied a prominent place in the room. The entire bedroom ceiling was mirrored. An additional mirror angled from the ceiling above the foot of the bed gave a lengthwise view, in addition to an overhead view, to the occupants of the bed. The bed itself was covered with a lace spread and strewn with goose down pillows of all shapes and sizes.

Large floor-to-ceiling windows took up half the space of the two outside walls. The space between the windows was also covered with mirrors. French doors opened onto a walled patio. The other two walls were covered with white fabric. Large expanses of the fabric were left starkly blank while other areas had been used as a canvas on which had been painted images depicting every imaginable form of sexual activity.

Rebecca looked at the bed, then at the mirrored ceiling. She glanced at the erotic paintings, trying not to linger on them. Her heart pounded in her chest as the sexual nature of every item in the room overwhelmed her senses. She closed her eyes, trying to shut out what she was seeing. She turned and ran toward the doors in a mindless attempt to escape the feeling of terror that enveloped her.

Edward moved quickly, reaching the doors before she did. Grabbing her arm he backed her up against a wall, pressing his body against hers. He spoke with absolute authority. "There will be no escape—not from me, not from this suite, not from this house and not from this island." He saw the tears well up in her eyes again.

"Come, Rebecca. There's more to see." He steered her toward a closed door. "This is the private bath." The sunken tub was designed to accommodate two people. The large, glass-walled shower had a total of six shower heads that sprayed from six different angles. A cupboard contained oversized, fluffy towels, bubble bath, scented oils, soaps, body lotions and various hair-care products.

They returned to the bedroom. "You'll notice a

phone in here and one in the sitting room. These phones are in-house only; you can't make an outside call from them. If there's anything you need just pick up the phone and ask."

Her manner was no longer defiant, just quiet and frightened. Her voice was barely audible. "How long do you plan to keep me a prisoner?"

He studied her, saw the anxiety in her eyes. "The length of your stay is entirely up to you. When you have proven yourself to be a sensuous, skillful and inventive lover who sincerely wants to please me, then I'll return you to Boston and your lifestyle there. In fact," he ran his fingertips across her cheek and down the side of her neck, "we might still be able to work out some type of agreeable financial arrangement. I'm no longer interested in reviving the contract I originally offered, but I'm sure something reasonable could be negotiated."

She was tired, almost beyond exhaustion. It had been a very long day and night, the emotional turmoil had taken its toll. His offer of money for sex, putting her in the category of a common whore, still incensed her, but she just didn't have the energy to argue with him about it. All she could say was, "I find your offer repugnant, and I find you repulsive beyond words." The statement was made without any sort of emotion or enthusiasm attached to it.

"In that case," his fingers nimbly untied the sash at her waist causing the robe to fall open, "we might as well get started." He ran his hands inside the robe and up over her shoulders, slipping the garment down her arms and off her body. He turned her to face one of the wall mirrors while he stood behind her.

"You have a very beautiful body, Rebecca." She moved her hands to cover as much of her nakedness as possible and closed her eyes, refusing to look at the reflection of him gazing at her nude body. Humiliation surged through her as she felt his hands pull hers away. "Look at it." It was a command, not a request.

She opened her eyes and watched in horror as his hands cupped the underside of her breasts. She had never seen, could not imagine, the sight of a man's hands holding her bare breasts. She was struck by the sharp contrast of his tanned skin against her porcelain coloring.

He moved his left arm around her, snuggled it tight up under her breasts. Then he closed his left hand over her right breast. He noted the trepidation on her face and felt her body tremble as her eyes closed. Her thighs pressed tightly together. His voice was sensual but firm. "Keep your eyes open, Rebecca. I want to make sure you watch everything that's going to happen."

Her tremors increased and the tears again welled up, but she kept her eyes open as she had been instructed to do. Edward's right hand traced the curve of her right hip. He forced his hand between her thighs, not yet touching the entrance he planned to penetrate very soon now. He felt her body tense as his fingers drew near her pussy lips. The tears overflowed her eyes and trickled down her cheeks. Her soft sobs reached his ears.

"Please, Edward…please don't do this to me. I…I can't…" She wanted to tell him that she didn't think, no matter how hard she tried or how much she wanted it to be so, that she would ever be capable of satisfying his sexual needs or wants.

"Yes, you can—and you will." He pushed his knee against the back of her thighs causing them to separate. He tickled his fingers over the silky moss adorning her mount and slowly moved one finger past her pussy lips and into her dry love tunnel. He moved his finger until he felt her juices start. "I can feel your dampness, your excitement, your desire. Don't deny yourself the pleasure—let go, enjoy."

He began to slowly slip his finger in and out of her while gently rubbing her clit with his thumb as he had done on the plane. "You know you like this, Rebecca. Don't lie to yourself—or to me. Look at how my finger moves in and out, in and out, in and out."

The same feelings that she had experienced on the plane started to swirl through her. He was making her feel things she had never felt before. Still she could no longer force herself to watch the vile act he was performing on her.

A hard sob escaped her throat. "Please don't do this to me. I can't do what you want, I can't be what you want. I don't know how. You were correct, I've never had an enjoyable sexual experience. In fact, I've not had any type of sexual experience since..." She couldn't bring herself to mention the horrible abuse she had suffered at Jason's hands. No one would ever know about that.

At least the rest of it was out; the secret she thought she would never reveal had been told to the last person in the world she ever wanted to have learn it. But now that he knew, now that he could understand her fears—well, surely he would let her go, would not force himself on her.

"Please let me go. I won't tell anyone about this. I won't make any trouble for you. Now that you know..."

He didn't stop what he was doing. It was as if he hadn't heard a word of her painful confession. His finger continued to slip in and out of her slit while his thumb continued to rub her clit.

Edward's could feel his hard cock straining against his jeans. He withdrew his hand from the warm nest it had found and released his hold on her. She sank into the softness of a chair and again covered her nakedness with her hands.

He quickly removed his own clothes, all the while talking to her. "Show me how you touch yourself, how you excite your pussy. Now, Rebecca—show me what it is that pleases you."

He saw her strong reaction to his words. Her face contorted into a strange, unreadable expression and she gasped. Her eyes widened in shock. She had trouble getting out any words at all. "I don't...I've never..."

He grabbed her arm, pulled her out of the chair and guided her toward the bed. Her body was trembling violently. This latest admission, that she had never masturbated, truly surprised him. Well, it had been quite an informative night. He hadn't realized just how much work this little adventure was going to require. It would have been easier if she were a virgin. At least that way she wouldn't have painful a past to overcome.

He stood behind her as she balked, refusing to get any nearer to the bed. He placed his hands on her waist and lifted her onto the bed, pinning her back against the softness of the pillows.

The sobs roiled through her body. "Don't do this, Edward. Please don't do this to me."

He ignored her words and inserted his knee between her legs, forcing them apart. Her hands balled into fists. She pushed frantically against his hard chest as she twisted her body, trying desperately to dislodge him.

The sting of his hand across her face shocked her into momentary submission. He had hit her; she didn't believe it could be possible, but it was true.

Edward's words were cold. "So, you still insist on doing it the hard way. You can't win."

Her face took on a look of defiance even though fear emanated from her eyes. "If you insist on violating me you're going to have to work for it. I'll never give in to you, even if you beat me."

He studied her for a moment as she continued to struggle beneath him. "As you wish. This could have been handled easily, but you've chosen the rougher road." He reached for the concealed velvet ropes attached to the bedposts. He quickly secured her wrists to the head of the bed. Next he trussed up her legs as he had on the plane. Rebecca frantically pulled at her bindings, her eyes full of fear, too frightened even to cry.

Edward cradled both her breasts in his hands, savoring the way her hard nipples pushed into his palms. His voice was very soft and sensual. "Now is the time, Rebecca. I'm going to fuck you. I'm going to jam my cock into your cunt. I know it's what you want…to feel my prick sliding in and out of your hot box." He slipped his finger past her pussy lips. She was dry again. He continued to work his finger around until he felt her dampness.

He lowered his head to the swell of her breast and licked the pebbled texture of her engorged nipple. She gasped; it sounded to him as though she tried to stifle a soft moan. He pulled the nipple into his mouth and began to suck. His own breathing became ragged as he moved his mouth to her other tit.

She didn't know what to do. Her mind told her to do whatever she had to do to stop this vile intrusion: to fight, hit, scratch—anything to make him know she wouldn't willingly allow him to violate her. She realized, however, that she was unable to put up a fight, to offer overtly physical resistance, tied up the way she was. What she did, therefore, was nothing. She neither cooperated nor resisted.

Edward moved his body over hers. He felt her jump and heard her gasp the moment the head of his enormous cock came in contact with her opening. "Now is the time, Rebecca. I'm going to fill your hungry pussy."

He teased her opening, rubbing his tool up and down against her inner pussy lips. He paused for a moment and focused on her face. There was still a red mark on her cheek where he had slapped her. He felt a twinge of remorse. Her eyes were squeezed shut, her lips pursed tightly together, a frown wrinkled her brow and her expression showed a mixture of dread and fear at the ordeal she was about to endure. Her fists were tightly clenched above her head.

"Rebecca, you can't enjoy the experience unless you relax." He resumed his teasing of her opening, barely penetrating her then pulling back. Her pussy was very tight, the tightest he had ever encountered. "Relax your muscles, you're all tensed up."

She didn't respond to his words. The moment she feared was here; he was going to ram his monstrous thing into her. He was going to have his way with her and then laugh at her. She tried to scoot away as he prodded her vaginal opening and pushed a little way inside before withdrawing, but her bindings prevented her.

He felt so big, so hard. She would never be able to accommodate all of him. Jason's penis had been small. After his initial rupturing of her maidenhead the pain had quickly subsided to be replaced by the physical feeling of him moving in and out of her. But there'd been no sensation. She had refused to date him again after that night, until she'd found out she was pregnant. If only he could have left it at that. But then, after they were married, he had brutally...

"Oh! Oh!" Rebecca's thoughts stopped, her eyes opened wide, her mouth opened to emit a startled gasp. Edward had swiftly and smoothly pushed all the way inside her with a single thrust. He completely filled her, stretched her sensitive membranes to the absolute maximum. She had never experienced anything like it. He was buried to the very root of his cock. His balls were resting against her upturned buttocks. She tried to catch her breath, to assimilate the very real physical things that were happening to her.

He quickly moved to capture her opened mouth, filling it with the thrusting of his tongue. At the same time he began to shuttle in and out of her tight pussy. He had never been inside anyone this tight. He felt her body tremble beneath him.

She may not have been willing to admit it, he thought, but he could feel how hot and wet she was. He needed to be very careful, to restrain himself. He wanted to force her to a level of excitement, to want more. But he didn't want her to achieve orgasm—not quite yet. He wanted to leave her hot, panting and unfulfilled. He wanted her to beg for him to continue.

"Move with me, thrust your hips up to meet my strokes. Come on, Rebecca. You can do it, you want to do it." His words tickled across her cheek and into her ear. He tangled his fingers in the pale golden tresses that spread out across the pillow.

She felt stirrings. She didn't want to feel them, didn't want them to exist. She didn't want him to be right. She forced herself to remain still. She wouldn't give him any satisfaction, the slightest hint of the truth of his words.

Her tight pussy squeezed his hard length more

than he wanted for what he was attempting to do. He didn't want to lose control, to succumb to the rush that slowly spread through his body. He captured her mouth with renewed intensity as he drove his cock deep into her cavern, silently demanding her cooperation.

Rebecca was in a complete state of confusion. She had been able to resist him—until he recaptured her mouth. His lips burned against hers, his insistent tongue took her breath away. She was scared—not only of him, but also of the strange things he was forcing her to feel.

Without a hint that he was going to do it, he pulled out of her and rolled over onto the bed. His abrupt actions startled her. She didn't understand why he had stopped. Then his words came back to her. She immediately understood...*until you beg me over and over again to fuck you into exhaustion, until your only desire in life is to willingly satisfy me in any and all ways, until you are able to completely fulfill my every fantasy no matter how depraved you may find it, until your every waking minute is consumed with your need for my cock...*

He saw the fire of recognition flare up in her eyes. His expression held no hint of his thoughts. His voice was soft. "It's been a long day and even a longer night. Perhaps some sleep is in order." He untied her. "Elsa will fetch you when it's time for breakfast." He glanced out the window at the first gray streaks of dawn. "Make that brunch."

She glared at him, her anger transcending her fear and confusion as it raged through her body. "You'll never have what you want! You'll never hear it from me, you bastard!" He caught her hand as she attempted to slap him.

She watched as he gathered his clothes and

walked out of the bedroom, his stiff cock bobbing up and down. She continued to watch as he walked across the sitting room and out the double doors, closing them behind him. She heard the click of the lock. Violent tremors raced through her, a combination of her rage at his cruel game and her frustration over the confusion coursing through her.

She turned over and buried her face in one of the pillows. He hadn't laughed at her, but the humiliation was every bit as great. He had tied her up, forced her to feel things, then coldly turned his back on her. She cried herself to sleep, not even bothering to cover her nude body.

Edward moved quickly down the hall and into the central section of the villa. He stopped in front of a door, punched a code number on the keypad lock, then entered the room. Elsa and Gunthar were sitting at a console watching one of several video monitors. The screen displayed one of several views of Rebecca's bedroom. She could be seen and heard as the sobs wracked her body.

Gunthar looked up at him as he entered the room, not even mildly surprised at his naked state or his hard erection. "Well?"

"Did she try to finish off the job after I left?"

"No, she never touched finger to pussy. She just started crying."

"We have lots of work to do. We failed to consider certain things that never showed up in the background search and things that—" He stopped in the middle of his sentence and turned to Elsa, giving her a quick wink and a grin. "Take care of this for me, sweetheart. It doesn't seem to want to go away on its own." He grabbed his still-hard cock and playfully wiggled it while thrusting his hips toward her.

FOUR

Edward returned his attention to Gunthar. "As I was saying, there are things that still have to be drawn out of her, secrets still hidden deep inside her, inhibitions that need to be overcome."

Elsa dropped to her knees in front of Edward and wrapped her lips around his erection. She knew exactly what he wanted at that moment. He wanted quick relief for his throbbing cock. Her mouth slid up and down his shaft while her hand cupped and gently massaged his balls. She gave him as quick and as efficient a blow job as was possible under the circumstances, taking him fully down her throat and massaging his turgid shaft with her muscles. She worked her gullet around his thick tool, expertly breathing through her nose and disregarding the gagging reflex.

She finally released him and took his jerking cock in both hands, then began to pump him while she licked the swollen head. Her tongue flicked out and lashed the gasping slit in the tip of his helmet. Edward grunted in response and thrust his hips forward. Pleased by his reaction, Elsa again took most of his shaft in her mouth and closed her lips around his girth as she fondled his balls. Her head bobbed back and forth quickly as she brought him to orgasm.

Edward's chest heaved as he tried to control his ragged breathing. He felt the rush start in his balls and move up through his body. The spasms began and his hot cream shot into her mouth in four great gouts. She continued to suck him until he finally withdrew from her mouth. Drops of his glistening semen clung to her lips; her eyes burned with excitement.

Elsa turned her attention to Gunthar, her breathing a staccato rasp. She pressed her mouth to his and purred excitedly as Gunthar licked the droplets of Edward's cream from her lips. She anxiously rubbed her hand over the bulge in Gunthar's pants.

"I can see there won't be any more business discussion for a while," said Edward. He watched as Gunthar pulled off her shorts, revealing a profusion of red pussy fur with an engorged clit poking its head out and her wetness already showing. Edward's cock stood at attention again.

Sexual energy filled the room. Elsa sank to the floor as Gunthar quickly removed his clothes. Before he was completely nude, Edward stepped in and buried his mouth in Elsa's hot cunt. He lapped at her freely flowing juices, nibbled on her protruding pussy lips and took her clit into his mouth.

Elsa screamed with delight as Edward began to suck on her hard love button. No sooner had he taken it into his mouth than he shoved three fingers up her pussy and moved them about in a manner that he knew drove her wild. She writhed and squirmed in ecstasy, all the while moaning and whimpering. Then he administered the final touch, thrusting his little finger all the way up her anus. He kept her impaled this way for several minutes, wriggling his fingers around and thrusting them in and out. Elsa shot over the edge into a massive orgasm.

When she slipped into a third intense orgasm, Edward pulled his hand away and quickly rammed his hard cock all the way into the depths of her convulsing pussy. Her love muscles locked onto his shaft and squeezed as wave after wave coursed through her. Still buried inside her, Edward raised himself up on his knees and pulled Elsa to him by the hips. He leaned forward and drew her legs over his shoulders, thereby opening her pussy to him even more. He drove into her mercilessly, becoming uncontrollably excited at the sight of his rigid cock drilling into her slit.

Elsa murmured to him the entire time, telling him how much she loved having his hard cock deep inside her love tunnel, how he was pounding into her so hard it felt as though his tool was going to emerge from her mouth. She grasped each time Edward sank into her and took one of her nipples into his mouth before he drew back and steadied himself for the next plunge.

Edward folded her legs back against her chest as he pistoned away like a man gone mad. His cock was near to bursting. He emitted a soft moan as another helping of his cream spurted into her.

They both remained very still for a few minutes as

they caught their breath, Edward's cock still embedded in Elsa's hot pussy. A moment later a new sensation tickled his balls as Gunthar softly lapped at the combined semen and pussy juice that seeped out around the place where Edward's cock joined Elsa's cunt.

After allowing a brief tremor of pleasure to course through him, Edward withdrew and stood up. "You two can fuck your brains out. I'm going to get some sleep. I've been awake for a little over twenty-four hours now and I'm tired. My original plan was to go back to Boston tomorrow morning and then return in a week, but the new information that's come to light dictates that I stay for a while longer. We'll revamp the game plan later today." Edward left the room.

Gunthar checked the monitor showing Rebecca's room. She was sound asleep. He turned his attention to Elsa. She lay before him, her legs spread invitingly wide apart. A surge of excitement shot through him when he saw her juices and Edward's cream trickling down her inner thigh. He had a raging hard-on that demanded relief.

Gunthar sat in a chair and held his pole upright. Elsa immediately climbed on him, lowering her dripping pussy onto his stiff shaft. He buried his mouth between her breasts and hungrily drew her right nipple between his lips. She moaned and sensually rocked back and forth on his lance, her sensitive clit rubbing hard against his pubic bone while her pussy muscles grabbed at his cock. He reached around her and wiggled his finger deep inside her anus. Elsa straightened up, arching her back so that her lush breasts were thrust more fully into Gunthar's face. He sucked her nipple thirstily, all the while working his finger in and out of her asshole. She continued to rock against him, drawing his cock into her gaping maw as far as it would go.

Gunthar gasped as he licked around her stiff peaks, teasing the dark flesh until it stood fully engorged. He could feel the heat rising from his balls into his belly and to the very tip of his throbbing shaft. His cock was twitching inside Elsa's insistent cunt; she was milking him expertly, bringing his juices to a boil and encouraging them to spill over. It wouldn't take much more of this kind of treatment. Gunthar smiled. His head lolled back and his eyes rolled up in his head as Elsa closed the muscles of her twat tightly around his lance for a series of strokes. Suddenly she put her feet on the floor and began to raise and lower herself, impaling her body on the full length of his cock. It sent Gunthar over the edge. His eruption began and spilled over into her waiting receptacle. He was groaning audibly as he grasped Elsa by the hips and started to move her to the rhythm of his frantic attack. He drove his burning poker into her, pumping out his unrestrained flood in great bubbling gouts. Swept away by his unbridled passion, Elsa released her own torrent, coating Gunthar's prick and mixing with his love juice until the overabundance of fluid spilled past her opening and onto his spasming thighs. Both were lost to the torrid waves that swept over them.

Edward seldom required more than four or five hours of sleep a night, if even that. Though it had been close to seven o'clock when he finally got to sleep, he was awake, showered, dressed and at work well before noon. First he took care of some business matters with his office in Boston, had his secretary fax him some files, and rescheduled his appointments for the rest of the week. He had a quick conversation with his pilot, then a meeting with Elsa. Having taken care of that, he and Gunthar strolled over to the tennis courts for a set before brunch.

They discussed the necessary changes in the plan for Rebecca, Edward bringing Gunthar up to date on as much of her sexual history as he had been able to discern since abducting her. "I want to know the reasons for her stark terror when I touched her asshole. It was far more than just being afraid; it had obviously already been penetrated several times. This will be Elsa's assignment. Get close to her, gain her confidence and find out what happened. She can use whatever method she finds prudent as long as it gets quick results and doesn't set back our efforts."

The two men became involved in their tennis game and set aside all other concerns. They had long been rivals on the courts, being evenly matched and excellent players.

Rebecca was still in bed. She had been awake for a while but had no desire to get up. She didn't want to face Edward. She didn't want to face this new day, didn't want to know what new games and humiliations it would bring.

She didn't know how long she had slept or what time it was, she only knew she was still tired. She was also slightly sore. It had been several years since anything had penetrated her most private intimacy, and Edward's proportions had definitely stretched it, both the opening and the interior walls.

Her moment of quiet was shattered by the opening of the bedroom door and the entrance of Elsa. "Good morning, Rebecca." She smiled pleasantly. "It's time to get up. I'll run a bath for you." She paused as she looked quizzically at the apprehensive woman. "Or would you rather have a shower?"

"It doesn't matter." Rebecca's attitude was very downcast, almost withdrawn.

Elsa continued in a light, upbeat manner. "I think I'll run you a bath. My guess is you're probably a little sore this morning. Edward is very well-endowed. Sitting in a nice tub of water will probably feel very soothing." The words were said in a very offhanded manner as if they were merely part of everyday conversation. Their purpose, however, was to see what type of response they would elicit.

Rebecca gasped in shock, turned a bright red and looked away, unable to make eye contact with Elsa. The response told Elsa what she wanted to know. Sex was a subject of embarrassment to Rebecca even as part of a "girl-to-girl" conversation. It was obvious that any personal sexual situation mortified her. When Edward had tagged her as "frigid" he had been on target.

Elsa continued to smile pleasantly as she went to the bathroom and started the water. She added some scented bath oil. While waiting for the tub to fill she made a quick determination of how she would proceed. Her intention was to continue to engage in casual conversation that incorporated as much discussion of sex as possible. She would treat it as if it were the most natural thing in the world—which to Elsa was the truth.

She returned from the bathroom and went straight to the walk-in closet and selected some clothes for Rebecca to wear. She chose a bright blue tank top and pair of shorts, no bra or panties. "Here you are, I'm sure you'll find these comfortable. By the time you've bathed and dressed brunch will be ready. Edward and Gunthar are on the tennis court."

She picked up the red robe from the end of the bed and tossed it into a laundry chute. "Just put your dirty clothes here. They'll be collected every day and returned laundered. Now," she stepped aside and waved her arm toward the bathroom, "this way to your bath."

Rebecca was hesitant about getting out of bed. During the course of the night she had pulled back the lace spread and covered herself with the sheet. She had nothing on and Elsa had just removed the robe from her reach. She would have to walk across the room completely naked in front of this stranger.

"Come on, Rebecca. Out of bed. Surely you can't be embarrassed about me seeing you without clothes. You don't have any body parts that are unique to you and you alone, do you? I mean, you don't have anything different than what I see when I look at myself in the mirror."

What Elsa said was true, reflected Rebecca. When she put it like that it did seem silly for her to be embarrassed. She slowly turned back the sheet and stepped out of bed. She went quickly to the bathroom and closed the door. She settled herself into the warm, soothing tub.

It was all Elsa could do to suppress her excitement at the sight of Rebecca's body. Such firm, round breasts. And that delightfully mossed pussy! Edward had been right again. Being able to enjoy the pleasures of that body would be worth a little extra effort. She felt a surge of excitement tickle her clit.

She tried to keep her mind on business. She opened the doors leading to the private patio, letting in the balmy, tropical air. She straightened the bed. The tingling in her clit refused to subside. She glanced toward the closed bathroom door, removed her jogging shorts and hopped up on the large bed.

She rubbed her clit between her finger and thumb, purring softly as the desired sensations washed over her.

As her excitement increased she reached her other hand between her legs and thrust two fingers deep inside her wet pussy. She felt her impending orgasm as she writhed about on the bed, rubbing her clit and thrusting her fingers in and out of her opening.

She heard the bathroom door open followed by Rebecca's loud gasp of shock. It didn't matter, because it was far too late for her to stop. She increased her efforts, and in a matter of moments she was deep in the throes of her climax. Nothing else mattered except the delicious waves surging through her body.

When Elsa recovered she slid off the bed and looked at Rebecca, who stood by the bathroom door wrapped in a large towel. Shock and disgust had transformed Rebecca's face. Elsa treated the entire incident as if it were an everyday occurrence, something she pretended to assume was also an everyday occurrence for Rebecca. "With Gunthar and Edward on the tennis court and my pussy aching for attention, I had to satisfy the urge myself—you know how it is."

Elsa passed her and entered the bathroom. "I'll be right back. I need to clean up the pussy juice that's starting to run down my thighs. I usually have someone give me a tongue bath, but right now I seem to be on my own," she paused and shot a questioning look toward Rebecca as she ran her index finger across the glistening moisture, "unless you'd want to…" She allowed her voice to trail off.

Rebecca's face clearly registered her horror at what she had just witnessed and what Elsa had said. She had trouble finding words to express her distaste.

"Of all the vile activities… how could you suggest… what type of perverted…sinful actions…?"

Elsa projected an air of innocent surprise at Rebecca's reaction. "My goodness, such an outburst. I'm amazed. Are you trying to say you don't pleasure yourself when the urge strikes, have never enjoyed the sensation of someone giving you a tongue bath, or…" she allowed a slight frown to wrinkle her brow, "…that you've never delighted to the attentions of another woman?"

Rebecca's face flushed crimson. "How could you even suggest something so…so unnatural."

"Unnatural? You think it's unnatural to enjoy the pleasures of the body just because you don't happen to have a partner at the moment, or the available partner is of the same gender? Have you really led that sheltered a life?"

Tears welled in Rebecca's eyes and sobs choked her throat. "Why are you talking to me like this, suggesting these terrible things to me?"

Elsa walked back out of the bathroom and stood very close to Rebecca. Her voice was soft and soothing as she put her arm around the sobbing woman's shoulder and steered her toward a chair. "There, there—don't be so upset. Sit down for a moment and collect yourself."

Rebecca composed herself while Elsa stood patiently in front of the chair with her legs parted. As Rebecca took several deep breaths to calm herself, she became aware of a scent that was new to her. She didn't look up at Elsa, afraid to meet her gaze.

Rebecca's senses had suddenly become very alive. She was aware that the scent emanated from Elsa's private place, the scent of her womanhood. She flashed on the mental image of Edward inhaling the fragrance from the crotch of her panties while they were on the plane. She allowed her gaze to travel from the floor up Elsa's shapely legs to her hairy mound. She saw the wet secretions matted in the mass of red fur. She had an almost uncontrollable desire to reach out and touch the moisture. She allowed a quick intake of breath as she quelled the forbidden impulse.

Elsa sensed what was happening—what she had hoped would happen. She spoke in a soft, soothing tone of voice. "Would you like to touch me? It's all right, go ahead."

Rebecca finally looked up at Elsa's face. Her heart pounded and her throat felt dry. This was all so sinful, so perverted. She saw Elsa's sincere smile of encouragement. A feeling of acceptance and understanding settled over her. She didn't feel that Elsa was trying to humiliate or degrade her.

Elsa continued to encourage her. "Please touch me, Rebecca." She called her by name as often as she could, knowing the sound of her own name would make Rebecca feel more comfortable. "I would enjoy experiencing your touch. I won't touch you unless you want me to. Don't be afraid."

Rebecca swallowed several times, trying to diminish the lump in her throat. She slowly reached her trembling hand toward Elsa's damp bush. With very tentative, unsure motions she touched her index finger to the wet fur, then to Elsa's engorged clit protruding through the hair.

Elsa jumped as Rebecca's hesitant touch came in contact with her sensitive clit. She saw Rebecca's eyes widen.

Rebecca quickly withdrew her hand, her gaze automatically dropping to the floor. She finally stammered, "I'm sorry...I didn't mean to...I mean, I'm sorry if I hurt..."

"No, no, you didn't hurt me, Rebecca. My clit is always very sensitive right after an orgasm. Surely you must have experienced the same thing, haven't you?" She saw the confusion and uncertainty in Rebecca's eyes.

"Rebecca? Does that look mean that you've never had an orgasm? Not even when you've pleasured yourself? How can that be? Edward didn't bring a virgin here, you've had experience. How is it possible?"

Elsa saw the pain and humiliation come into Rebecca's eyes. Her mind worked quickly to sort things out. Was this the right time to push her for answers, or should she back off and let Rebecca enjoy her minor accomplishment? She decided to retreat for the moment and give Rebecca some breathing room.

She reached her hand out to Rebecca. "Come on, get up and get dressed while I clean up. Brunch is ready. We'll have time to talk later."

Edward and Gunthar were already seated at the table when Elsa escorted Rebecca to the dining room. Elsa gave them a quick look indicating progress was being made—a look not noticed by Rebecca. The two men rose to their feet, and Edward held the chair for Rebecca as she sat down.

"Good morning, Rebecca. Did you sleep well and find everything you needed this morning?" Edward's voice was upbeat and cheerful, as if nothing out of the ordinary was happening. "I trust Elsa is seeing to your necessities."

Rebecca was unable to meet his gaze. Her response was uttered without any enthusiasm. "I suppose so." Gunthar added a cheery greeting to Rebecca who could only manage a mumbled "hello" in response.

As soon as everyone was seated, brunch was served. Rebecca's surprise at the quality of the meal clearly showed on her face. There was salmon mousse with dill sauce, artichoke hearts with vinaigrette dressing, fresh fruit and pastry. She ate in silence as she listened to Edward and Gunthar discuss the merits of the morning's tennis and tend to some business concerning the village on the other side of the island.

At the mention of the village, Rebecca's head jerked up and her attention became riveted on the conversation. *So, this compound is not the only thing on the island. There is a village and people.*

Edward caught her quick snap to attention. "Yes, Rebecca. There are people who live on the island all the time. Some are my employees, others are natives who have always lived here. Don't get your hopes up. None of this will be of any help to you. You're free to roam the grounds within the compound walls during the day and will have free access to most of the villa. That's it unless you're in the company of Elsa, Gunthar, or myself."

She sat back in her chair and sipped her coffee. The little flicker of hope had been immediately crushed. She would remain Edward's prisoner—what was it he had called her, his *captive*?—for as long as he wanted, until she was able to perform to his satisfaction all the vile acts he wanted. She closed her eyes and the overwhelming immensity of her plight swept over her.

"Rebecca?" She jumped at the sound of Edward's voice coming from behind her. She had been so preoccupied with her own thoughts she had failed to notice him leave his seat and move to her chair. He held out his hand to her. "Let me show you the villa and the grounds." She refused his hand, but stood up and prepared to follow him.

Gunthar watched them leave then looked questioningly at Elsa as he pulled her onto his lap. "Well?"

"What we have is a sexually repressed woman who, in the past twenty-four hours, has had her eyes and consciousness opened to more things than she ever realized existed. All of it scares the hell out of her. Edward was right on target with his reassessment."

Gunthar slipped his hand up the leg of her shorts and ran his finger along the edge of her clit before inserting it into her wet opening. His voice grew husky as he attempted to discuss business. "We made it to security control just in time to hear you talking about a tongue bath with Rebecca." He withdrew his finger and put it in his mouth, sucking her juices. "Are you still interested?"

"Will Edward be needing us right away, or is he planning another session with Rebecca?"

"He plans to be busy with her until dinner. We're free until they vacate her suite, then we have to activate the speakers and screens." Gunthar chuckled softly. "He wants to have the tape of Randall Carpenter standing by—that should shock her sensibilities and knock her notions of 'well-bred, socially acceptable, proper background' right into the toilet."

Elsa glanced at her watch. "It looks like we have quite a bit of time to ourselves." She flicked her tongue across his lower lip. "Let's see if we can't find something worthwhile to do to occupy that time." She practically ripped the clothes from his body, staring admiringly as his stiff cock sprang free and bobbed before her, anxious for attention.

Gunthar reciprocated, tearing Elsa's shorts and top from her body. He licked her neck and shoulders before descending to the tantalizing valley between her breasts. He kneeled in front of her, drawing her nipples into his mouth and raking them with his teeth until they became dark and swollen. Then he pulled her to her knees and turned her around, easing her onto the carpeted floor. He pushed her onto her belly and spread her legs with a single sweep of one knee. With a practiced motion he slid between her thighs and brought the thick head of his cock to her slit from behind. He began to push into her, rearing back from the hips and thrusting forward until half his length was lodged in her tight tunnel.

He loved doing it this way; he loved the feel of her soft ass against his belly as he pushed and pushed. With a final thrust, he buried himself inside her to the balls and began shuttling in and out. She was so tight, so juicy. He reached around and grabbed her swaying breasts, cupping the mounds and rolling the nipples between his fingers. He knew Elsa liked it this way as well. She had told him many times in the past how she could feel every inch of his large cock scraping the walls of her pussy as he plunged to the center of her cavern. This time was no exception, Gunthar reflected with satisfaction. Elsa was writhing beneath him, murmuring wordlessly and thrusting back against him, urging him to fuck her hard. He smiled. Her wish was his demand.

Edward showed Rebecca through the living room, the library, the solarium, the gym, the kitchen, finally ending up in the entertainment room with its large-screen television with VCR, stereo equipment and enough empty floor space to dance.

The entertainment room opened onto a large patio which extended down toward the swimming pool and then beyond to the tennis courts. He guided her around the corner of the house to a private patio, opened the French doors and entered a large master bedroom.

"This is my bedroom, Rebecca. I hope you like it because you will eventually be spending a significant amount of time here." He felt her flinch at his mention of what he intended.

Her gaze slowly traveled around the room. She was pleasantly surprised by what she saw. The room was very attractive and tastefully decorated. It was decidedly masculine, yet still retained a comfortable warmth. Her tone of voice carried her amazement. "This isn't at all what I would have expected. It's really very…" She realized she was about to say something nice and stopped talking.

He placed his hands on her shoulders and turned her to face him. "You have too many preconceived notions about things. You have to learn to experience things…and people…as they really are, not how you think they are going to be or should be. Life isn't one neat little package where everything is exactly as you would like it to be all the time."

She tried to step back from him, but he tightened his grip on her shoulders, refusing to let her escape his touch. Her voice and face became defiant. "Isn't that exactly what *you're* doing, demanding that everything be just the way you want it?"

He studied her for a long moment, his silver eyes piercing her. She felt the heat of his energy, the magnitude of his power and passions. It frightened her. He was definitely unlike anyone she had ever known. His magnetism held her to him; she was unable to look away. She felt her heart pound. She didn't want it to be so, but it was.

Finally he spoke in answer to her taunt, his voice very soft. "No, Rebecca. That's not what I'm doing."

She trembled as she felt his hand move down her

back and across her bottom. His fingers trailed across the curve of her perfectly-rounded cheeks. Then he grasped her by the ass and pulled her hard against him, absolutely overwhelming her with the power of his heated passion.

In one swift motion his mouth captured hers. He forced his tongue between her lips, though they were not so tightly pursed together this time. He felt her defiance and resistance as she attempted to push away from him. He held her tightly until she stopped struggling. His fingers sensually stroked her through the fabric of her shorts until they arrived at the elastic waistband. He slipped his hands inside the shorts, reveling in the silky texture of her bare bottom.

He cupped her rounded buttocks and teased the separation of her cheeks with his fingers. He felt her body stiffen as she tried to pull away from him again, her actions becoming frantic as he held her tightly. He could feel her rising panic as she struggled in his arms.

Suddenly he released her from his hold. He stood back and looked at her. Her hardened nipples stood out in stiff peaks against the fabric of her tank top. Her breathing was ragged. Her face was flushed. He was satisfied with what he saw.

He grabbed her hand and headed toward his bedroom door. "Come on, Rebecca. It's time to continue where we left off last night." Without another word he pulled her along behind him and entered the next door down the hall—her suite.

They passed quickly through the sitting room and into her bedroom. He closed the door and turned to face her. "Take off your clothes." Without another word he removed his tennis shoes and socks, his tennis shorts and shirt, then his briefs. She stood there, not making any effort to comply with his order.

He again followed his command with decisive action. He pulled the tank top over her head then pulled the shorts down to her ankles. "Step out of them, now!" His voice was firm but not angry. She finally complied with his wishes.

He steered her toward the bed. "You have only the rest of today and tomorrow to familiarize yourself with the basics of lovemaking. After that Gunthar will take over, fine-tuning your skills until he thinks you're ready for my final inspection." He watched as shock came into her eyes.

"You mean...not only am I forced to submit to you, but I'm also expected...?" Tears welled in her eyes, and panic covered her face. Her voice was tiny and frightened. "Is there no end to the humiliation you intend to inflict on me?"

"I don't inflict humiliation on you, Rebecca. You create it yourself. You'll find Gunthar very skillful in an impressive variety of pleasures." As far as Edward was concerned, the conversation was over. He picked her up and placed her in the middle of the bed, then stretched his body out next to hers, his hard cock bobbing in the air

Rebecca tried to struggle out of his grasp but he quickly pinned her body to the bed, holding her arms stretched above her head. His voice was hard, impatient. "Do you want me to tie you up again?" His tongue dabbed at her hardened nipple, then he took it in his mouth and sucked as he released her arms. She knew if she continued to struggle he would do as he promised. She closed her eyes, her arms stiff at her sides and her legs clamped together.

The pebbled texture of her taut nipple stimulated his desire. He quickly captured her other nipple in his mouth, teasing it to a hard peak. He slid his hand smoothly down her rib cage, over her hip and between her thighs, cupping her mound while being careful not to penetrate past her pussy lips.

Edward's voice was soft and sensual. "I can feel your heat, Rebecca. I can feel your passion. Let go." He inserted his finger between her delicate little lips. "Go with your desires, don't deny yourself the pleasure." He teased her clit with his thumb as he inserted a second finger. "Your juices are flowing. You're hot and wet for me, you want me." He continued to manipulate her pussy while his mouth roved over her nipples.

Rebecca's body was on fire. She wanted to remain still, let him perform his vile deeds without giving him the satisfaction of knowing she felt something. Her breathing quickened, then became very ragged.

"That's it, Rebecca. I can feel the years of pent-up passion surging through your body. Your pussy is so hot and so very wet." He increased his stimulation of her clit, moved his fingers enticingly inside her love tunnel, then forced his tongue between her closed lips and deep into her mouth. Her resistance felt like more of a token gesture than anything else.

Rebecca could hardly think. Her attempts at making some sort of logical determination about what was happening to her were simply washed away by the power of her long-buried passions. To her shame and embarrassment, she had to admit he was right...she wanted more. She wanted him inside her again, to fill her as he had done the night before.

She tried not to respond to his kiss, but the forbidden delights she had sampled so many years ago, a time prior to Jason's forced intercourse with her, came back in a flood of exhilaration. She tentatively responded to his kiss. She allowed her fingers to skim across his bare shoulder.

The door had been opened; she was unable to

close it. She ran her fingers through his thick hair, then circled her arms around him. Her hips moved, almost imperceptibly at first, then in a rhythmic motion pushing harder against his hand as his fingers excited her. His thumb caused the most intense sensations she had ever experienced.

She wasn't sure what was happening to her. Her heart pounded in her chest, and she couldn't catch her breath. She grabbed frantically at him, pulling his body closer to hers, pushing harder against his hand. She whimpered and moaned as her senses raced toward oblivion. Then reality came rushing back, and her senses abruptly shut down. Her movements stopped.

"Damn!" Edward whispered the word softly under his breath, his disappointment at what had happened clearly evident. He had been so sure she was going to have her first orgasm. She had been almost there, then her subconscious fears had slammed the door shut. Until she was able to experience her own sexuality and fully enjoy all facets of lovemaking, she wouldn't be capable of being his perfect lover. He didn't want someone who just went through the motions. He wanted someone whose excitement would match his own.

Her whimpers and moans of joy turned into sobs of frustration. Tears ran down her cheeks. She knew something very powerful had been about to happen. She had wanted it to happen. She had never before experienced anything like what he had created in her. Then it had all stopped.

Her eyes were filled with bewilderment and confusion as she searched his face for answers. He left his fingers inside her passion-swollen pussy and continued to gently manipulate her engorged clit. He took special care to make sure his voice held no hint of reprimand. It was not a time for anger or punishment. She had tried, had cooperated. He brushed his lips softly against hers. "What happened, Rebecca? You were so close to experiencing the greatest of pleasures. Was it something I did? Did I touch a spot that caused you pain?"

She was unable to hold his gaze. She didn't know how to answer his questions because she didn't know what had happened. She wanted to have the sensations back, but they just weren't there.

Her voice was hollow and filled with an unmistakable anguish and disappointment. "I told you I couldn't do what you wanted, could never be what you wanted. I don't know how. I tried, but I'm just not capable." The tears streamed down her cheeks. Her words were not defiant or angry; they were honest and showed the depth of her despair.

Edward considered his options. He could continue with his manual stimulation, he could insert his cock into her eager cunt, he could introduce her to the wonders of oral sex, or he could give her a little while to compose herself before continuing.

He looked at her tear-streaked face and saw something new, a sadness that had not been there before—a genuine disappointment. He smiled inwardly. *She'll come around real soon now. She's trying; she wants to try.*

He determined to stay on the island until she was able to easily achieve orgasm. It was a setback he had not originally anticipated. It would require a more intense schedule, longer sessions, more work. He wondered if she had the stamina for what was ahead, for the immensity of the undertaking.

Edward slowly removed his hand from her love nest and sensually brought one of his dripping fingers to his mouth, all the time carefully watching her reaction. "You taste as sweet as honey. You're going to be a very enjoyable feast." He saw her eyes widen in shock. "Here, sample your delicious nectar." Her head jerked away from him as he extended his hand toward her.

Rebecca caught a whiff of the same type of scent she had experienced with Elsa. She was both repulsed and curious. He had actually tasted what was down there in her private place and seemed to enjoy it. Then she remembered Elsa's words about a tongue bath. She was abruptly brought back to the present when Edward shoved his pussy-soaked finger into her mouth.

FIVE

"Suck on it, Rebecca. Taste your sweet spicing. Learn to enjoy the taste. There will be many new tastes and textures in your life. Suck on my finger. Very soon you'll learn to suck on something far more substantial." His words jarred her senses.

She didn't know what to think or feel. She wanted to be repelled by his actions and words, but to her dismay she wasn't. The odd taste of her own secretions wasn't really offensive—in fact, it was kind of intriguing. The feel of his finger in her mouth caused a tremor of excitement. She found herself doing as she was told, gently sucking on his finger until all the honey had been consumed. Then she felt his other hand between her legs.

His stimulation of that special place spurred her actions. Even though the taste was gone, she sucked harder and harder on his finger. She felt the marvelous sensations again building in her body. She welcomed them, she wanted them. Her tongue aggressively swirled around his finger, and she sucked even harder.

Her logic and sense of reality slipped away. She moved her hands up and rolled her hardened nipples between each thumb and forefinger while her palms cupped the underside of her firm globes. She had never before touched herself in this manner. Her hips thrust against Edward's hand encouraging him into a faster rhythm.

He was very pleased. His eyes beheld a beautiful woman writhing in the throes of sensual delight, whimpering and moaning with pleasure. He nudged her hand away from one of her nipples and took the taut peak into the warmth of his mouth. He immediately emulated the sucking rhythm she was using on his finger. He wanted to plunge his throbbing cock into her, wanted to fuck her senseless. He held off, not wanting to break the rhythm that had her so excited, not wanting to interrupt her pending orgasm.

All her senses were on fire. Both her mind and body were overwhelmed by the incendiary waves that coursed through her. Then it happened. Something exploded deep inside her and spread outward. She skyrocketed to a place she had never imagined even existed. It was the most powerfully overwhelming sensation of her life. She cried out in ecstasy as the waves crashed over her.

Edward's breath came in ragged puffs. As soon as Rebecca started convulsing he rammed two fingers all the way into her hot cunt and pushed the heel of his hand hard against her throbbing clit and held it there. He watched her face contort in the throes of her rapture. She was so beautiful. For the first time, she had surrendered her icy facade. A thin sheen of perspiration covered her skin, and strands of her hair stuck to the dampness on her face. Yes, all this extra effort was going to be worth it...she was exquisite.

Rebecca whimpered and cried as her body returned to earth and reality returned. She opened her eyes and looked at Edward. He saw confusion and embarrassment. Slowly he removed his two fingers from her dripping pussy, sucked her juices from one of them and offered her the other one. With a look of shy reluctance on her face, she took the wet finger into her mouth.

"Congratulations. You are now truly a woman. Those marvelous feelings you just experienced will be yours again and again in so many different ways." He gently parted her legs with his knee and situated himself between her thighs, his hard cock teasing her wet and tingling slit. His mouth captured hers as he thrust his pole all the way into her in one long stroke, the wetness of her pussy lubricating his penetration of her tight tunnel.

She tried to gasp as he completely filled her with his hardness. When she opened her mouth he just as smoothly thrust his tongue inside to twine with hers. She accepted the intrusion into both of her openings. His powerful cock sent sparks through her as he moved in and out of her tantalizing love canal.

She was so tight, so wet, so very hot. His belly slapped hers on the downstroke. She wasn't moving with him, but neither was she resisting. He had been so excited watching her experience her first orgasm that he didn't know how long he would be able to last. He drove into her with short thrusts that made her luscious tits bounce. He wanted to prolong this delicious torture as long as he could. He wanted to drive her to at least two more orgasms before he came. He wanted her to be so hot and hungry that she would beg him for more—as he had promised her she would. Once that had been achieved, then he would move on to more diverse pleasures.

He knew she was trying to hold back. He also knew she wouldn't be able to deny herself now that she had tasted ecstasy. He felt her pussy muscles grab his cock and her love tunnel begin to contract. He pulled all the way out until only his cock head remained between her pussy lips.

Her eyes opened wide with shock. She instinctively thrust her hips toward him and he skillfully moved away, always leaving only his engorged helmet parting her nether lips. Her movements became frantic as she tried to bring him back inside her. She even reached toward his cock with her hand but he deflected her aim. He saw the frustration building on her face and felt the tension in her body.

He had given her body a shock, suddenly pulling out of her when she was so close to orgasm. He continued to tease just her vaginal opening, rotating his hips and spreading the fleshy folds without delving inside. She wanted to experience everything again and again. She wanted the delicious sensations to reclaim her. Why was he teasing her like this, torturing her with his hard penis? She was doing what he wanted.

Somewhere in the back of her mind she realized what was going on, what he was doing and why, but she didn't care. He would have his way once again. She had vowed she would never beg him. She had been wrong.

"Please, Edward." Her voice trembled and her words were breathless. "Please don't do this to me. I'll do what you want, don't make me beg you."

"Beg me?" His voice contained a false innocence. "Why would you be begging me? What is it you want, Rebecca?"

"Please, Edward…" Her voice was barely audible.

"Please what?" He cupped one breast and manipulated her hard nipple and pushed his cock halfway in before quickly withdrawing it again. "Please what, Rebecca?"

She tried to thrust against him, take his length all the way in, but he was too adept at the game and she too inexperienced. "What, Rebecca? What is it you want?"

"Please, Edward." She whimpered as the tears ran down her cheeks. "Please…"

"You keep saying that but you don't tell me what it is you're asking for. What do you want, Rebecca? Say it."

Her words were mumbled; the frustrations coursing through her body were almost more than she could handle. "Please don't stop."

"I can't hear you. Say it louder."

Anger mixed with her frustrations as she glared at him, her body trembling with emotion. The words were said as convincingly as she could say them. "Don't stop. Please, continue."

His voice remained soft and sensual. "Don't stop what? Continue what? What is it you want, Rebecca?"

Her need erupted with volcanic ferocity. "FUCK ME! I'M BEGGING YOU! FUCK ME!"

A satisfied grin curled the corners of his mouth. "You don't need to shout." He slowly pushed his hard length all the way into her. "All you had to do was tell me what you wanted." He thought it was probably the first time in her life she had ever used the word "fuck."

He brought her frantic gyrations under control and set a smooth rhythm that quickly escalated until she exploded into orgasm, her pussy muscles squeezing his eager cock. He fought to maintain control as he propelled her immediately to another climax. Before that one could subside he rushed to his own rapture, his pelvis thrusting forward and pulling back as he banged her as hard as he could.

What he had told her on the plane had come true, Rebecca reflected. She had wanted what he was doing so much she had begged him not to stop. She hated him for what he had made her do, begging him and even using that vile word. She closed her eyes as shame coursed through her.

He wrapped his arms tightly around her and gave one final deep thrust. Then his body stiffened, and the spasms raced through him. His own orgasm was so powerful Rebecca actually felt his hot cream spurting deep inside her, felt his cock jump and twitch with each spurt.

Edward remained still, bringing his labored breathing under control and contemplating his next step. He slowly became aware of how warm and soft her body felt beneath his. Gone was the cold, stiff mannequin he had brought to the island. He slowly withdrew his diminishing cock from her dripping cunt. He had already decided what his next move would be.

He moved up her body until he straddled her shoulders. He watched as her eyes, once again, widened at the sight of his prick dangling right in front of her face. "You're going to have to learn to stop registering shock and disapproval at each new thing that happens. Your life is going to be filled with lots of new things."

Edward took his index finger, scooped up a bit of

the sticky mixture coating his staff and held it to her lips. "Here, Rebecca. Taste. It's a combination of your sweet pussy juices and my cream." He touched his finger to her lips and waited.

She turned her head aside, her shame and humiliation complete. He turned her head back. "We're not going through this reluctance to cooperate again, are we? Take my finger into your mouth, now."

Tentative and unsure about what to expect, she allowed him to slip his finger into her mouth. The sample was unusual but not distasteful. She recognized the taste of her own juices and was able to discern a different, slightly salty taste mixed with it. She sucked until it was gone then continued with little baby sucks until he withdrew his finger.

"Now for the real thing." He touched the tip of his revived cock to her parted lips. "Take it, savor it, lick it clean." He saw her uncertainty and confusion. She seemed not to know what to do or how to proceed. "It's just like my finger, only bigger. Use your tongue, lick off our combined juices, take the head into your mouth and suck on it." His breathing had quickened considerably. He nudged his hard organ against her lips. "Do it." The last words were a command, not a request.

Rebecca closed her eyes. She had already sunk to the level of the depraved by consuming her own secretions, using vile language to beg him to have sex with her, and even touching her own breasts in a sensual manner. Now this. How much more could there be before he was through with her, before he was satisfied with her degradation?

Her tongue made contact with his cock. She had never touched a penis before—not even with her hand—not even Jason's when they were married. The extreme hardness surprised her, as did the velvety texture of the head. She dabbed her tongue at the stickiness. The taste was becoming more enticing with each flick of her tongue. She willingly consumed all that was there.

After she had licked his cock clean she paused and again looked at him questioningly, seemingly unsure of how to carry out the rest of his command.

"Take my cock in your hand and hold it to your lips."

Her trembling fingers wrapped around the girth of his hard shaft. She stared at it but didn't move it to her mouth. She looked up at his impassive face. There were no fires of passion in his eyes, no signs of desire on his face—his expression was very matter-of-fact. Her voice quavered as she said: "I can't do this. It's too big. It won't fit into my mouth. It will choke me."

He studied her for a moment, considering her words and fears. Perhaps he would leave this part of the indoctrination to Gunthar whose cock wasn't as big as his. After she became accustomed to accommodating Gunthar it would be easier for her to handle him. It had been a long and intense session and she had already accomplished quite a bit that afternoon. But he wanted to try one more experiment before dinner.

"I'm a reasonable man, Rebecca. I'll let Gunthar introduce you to this pleasure. We'll move on to something else for now." He saw the trepidation move across her face. He quickly moved all the way down her body and situated himself between her legs. Then he ran his arms under her thighs and lifted her legs over his shoulders. Before Rebecca even knew it he had buried his face in her steaming crotch.

She didn't know what was happening or why. Suddenly her legs were across his shoulders and his face was snuggled up against her private place. She felt his hot breath coming in short bursts, tickling through her pubic patch. Her entire body quivered even though she had no idea what he was about to do to her.

The scent of her womanhood aroused his senses. He took a deep breath, inhaling her sweet odor. He felt her quiver as he exhaled across her pussy fur. She stimulated him more than he had imagined she could. When she learned all the intricacies of lovemaking, she would be the most exciting thing he had ever possessed.

He ran his tongue around her slit then nibbled at her delicate pussy lips. He dabbed and lapped at the sticky secretions that oozed from her. After drinking everything, he flicked his tongue across her clit.

He heard her gasp of surprise followed by a soft moan as he teased her opening with his tongue. Then he took her clit into his mouth and began to suck. At that precise moment Edward's entire world consisted of the sweet taste and tantalizing texture of the feminine folds of Rebecca's delicious pussy. He knew he would be spending many of the days, weeks, months, and maybe even years to come devouring this tasty treat.

A totally unexpected surge of electric energy shot through Rebecca's body the second Edward put his mouth to her cunt. It literally took her breath away, causing her to gasp for air. Her nerves tingled and danced as he titillated her senses. Her mind wasn't able to assimilate what was happening. She only knew she wanted more of this and hoped he wouldn't stop and make her beg for it. She thrust her mound hard against his mouth, grinding against his lips and tongue. Her hands cupped her breasts, rolled and teased her hard nipples.

Her immediate and enthusiastic response to his lingual ministrations delighted him. There was no hesitation on her part, no attempt to hold back. He felt the hot demands of her pussy as he added the sensation of his finger inside her love tunnel. As he worked the finger around, using it to open her slit as well as stimulate her, he darted his tongue into her tunnel, lashing the pink membranes that were now presented to him like dessert after a meal. He scoured the sensitive tissues, sometimes lapping at them, sometimes tickling them with the tip of his tongue. All the while Rebecca continued to thrust her mound against his mouth, as if insisting that he penetrate her more deeply and grant her even more of this startling new sensation. He was just as eager to show her the heights of ecstasy to which she could ascend. He added another finger to the first and began thrusting them in and out as his tongue bathed her outer folds. She exploded into one orgasm after another, her wetness spreading over his cheeks and chin as he lapped hungrily at her flowing juices.

Rebecca's body had been drawn into a swirling vortex, sucked down until she was gasping for air, pulled apart into a million fragments, each one alive with the intense sensations. She erupted into an unending orgasm. Her soft moans turned into screams as wave after wave of searing ecstasy crashed through her.

Her hands moved frantically about, squeezing her breasts and nipples, running up and down her sides and across her abdomen, then finally reaching for Edward's head, pulling his face tighter against her throbbing pussy as she bucked and ground against his mouth. She was beyond exercising any control over herself.

Elsa and Gunthar watched on the monitor. He

zoomed the picture in tight on her face. "Look at her." He grinned at Elsa. "It looks like you're not the only one who could spend the rest of her life having someone munch on her pussy. I'd say Edward has made quite a bit of progress since we parted company four hours ago."

Elsa's eyes glowed with excitement. She watched Rebecca's head thrash from side to side. "I can hardly wait until it's my turn to have her." She looked questioningly at Gunthar. "It *will* be soon, won't it darling?"

The sounds of Rebecca's ecstasy filled the speakers in the security room. Gunthar adjusted the picture so that it encompassed only the bed, not the entire room. Elsa stood behind Gunthar and slipped her arms around his waist and her hands down the front of his tennis shorts. She fondled his balls and lightly stroked his hardening cock.

Her voice held a hint of mock surprise. "My, my! I'm surprised you have this much energy left after that workout we had. Is there something I can do for you to relieve this condition?" She kissed his back as she continued to stroke him.

He looked away from the monitor and pulled her arms from around him as he turned toward her. "What you can do," he reached up the leg of her shorts, tickled his fingers through her abundant pussy fur and tweaked her clit, "is stop teasing my prick. We need to attend to business now. We'll have more time to play later tonight." He kissed her tenderly on the tip of the nose. "And yes, you'll have your turn with her very soon, possibly tonight."

He glanced back at the monitor just in time to see Edward plunge his cock deep into Rebecca's swollen pussy and commence hard, quick thrusts. Gunthar knew this signaled the end of the session; Edward was going for his own orgasm, no longer savoring the hot passions of leisurely lovemaking.

Just when Rebecca thought she would pass out from the intense sensations that rippled through her body, Edward removed his mouth from her love box and replaced it with his throbbing cock. Her body jerked and trembled as he plunged into her, ramming in and out like an untiring piston. He thrust his tongue deep into her mouth, filling her with the taste of her own juices. She sucked greedily on it and melted into the last of a long string of orgasms, her body totally drained of strength and energy.

Her eager acceptance of his tongue triggered the release of his last bit of control. Spasms raced through his body as he shot streams of hot cream inside her hungry pussy. His body collapsed on top of hers, his hand cupping her breast and lightly fingering her nipple.

The air was thick with the aroma of their sex and the sound of their breathing as they gasped for air. They both remained still, the only movement being his manipulation of her taut nipple. After a few moments he took her nipple into his mouth and gently sucked. She closed her eyes and purred softly, a contented smile curling the corners of her lips.

It was Edward who broke the silence. "Tell me, was that as enjoyable for you as it seemed? I hope so, because it's only the beginning. Now that you've learned to be a woman, you'll explore many other avenues of pleasure. It's time to prepare for dinner now, but we'll continue where we left off later."

Rebecca's voice contained something different. Gone was the cold edge. In its place was a quiet resignation, an acceptance of her fate. "Is this how you intend for me to spend the rest of my life, being your sex slave? Fucking you and sucking you all the time?"

He made no effort to get up off the bed, and she made no effort to move away from him. "There are far worse ways to spend your days and nights." He twined his fingers in her blond hair and lightly brushed her kiss-swollen lips with his tongue. "You'll be my lover, not my sex slave. There's a considerable difference between the two. A lover is a person, one who enjoys and enthusiastically participates. A sex slave is an object to which things are done.

"You have intelligence and education, two things I prize highly. What you are now learning is to be a sensual and sexual woman so that you can enjoy all the pleasures of the body as well as the mind."

She said nothing. She didn't know how to respond to what he had just said. On the plane she had been horrified at his stated intentions, now she wasn't so sure. She couldn't deny the fires of ecstasy he lit in her, the incendiary rapture she had just experienced, the craving for more and more of what he was doing to her. To her embarrassment and shame, she loved every bit of it.

Edward slowly stretched out his tall frame and slid out of bed. "Come on, Rebecca. It's almost time for dinner." He held out his hand to her, and this time she accepted it. They walked to the bathroom together.

He adjusted the temperature and spray of the shower, then stood aside as she stepped in, following closely behind her. Without saying a word he provocatively lathered her entire body, giving particular care to her swollen and sensitive pussy. He felt her quiver as she stood quietly, allowing him to minister to her.

He placed the soap in her palm and placed his

hand over hers. He guided her in a circular stroking motion, gliding the soap over his muscular chest, down his hard flat belly, then into the dark patch surrounding the base of his flaccid cock. He removed his hand and she continued the erotically earthy massage of his finely-tuned body.

At first tentatively, then with more confidence, she touched all of him. Her fingers tickled through the soapy lather that covered his skin. She touched his limp prick and felt it twitch. She cradled his balls, something she had never done. She even allowed herself the thrill of running her hand over his bare bottom.

A slight frown wrinkled her brow as she thought of his words. He would be leaving, and Gunthar would take over. She would be required to have sex with Gunthar, all kinds of sex at all times. A cold chill settled over her even as the warm spray of the shower washed away the lather.

Edward and Rebecca appeared on the dining patio, both dressed in shorts and tank tops. It was a beautiful night, and he had instructed that dinner be served outdoors. They were leisurely enjoying a glass of wine when they were joined by Elsa and Gunthar.

Edward shot them a questioning look, and they responded with subtle nods. He smiled and returned his attention to Rebecca. Dinner progressed pleasantly, Gunthar and Elsa commenting on how much calmer Rebecca seemed than when she had arrived.

Rebecca blushed at the comments and was unable to hold their gaze. She knew there was no use in her pretending that they didn't know everything that had been happening and what was going to happen. She silently wondered what she would have to endure at Gunthar's hands while Edward was away.

After dinner Edward led her back to her suite. She removed her clothes without being told and settled into the softness of the bed. He removed his clothes and joined her.

Edward stretched out on his back and placed his hands on her hips. "Straddle me, sit on my face. I want to feast on your sweet pussy for dessert."

She felt the flush of embarrassment cover her cheeks. She also felt a surge of excitement flood her love nest as she recalled the torrid pleasures his mouth had brought to her that afternoon. With only a moment's hesitation she did as she was instructed. The warmth of his breath sent tremors of anticipation through her body.

He grasped her hips and lowered her quivering love box to his mouth. Heat radiated from her wet pussy. He touched the tip of his tongue to her clit and thrilled to the quick spasms that shot through her. She was still in a state of readiness, sensitive and stimulated. His teeth gently nibbled at her tender pussy lips, then he covered her clit with his mouth and thrust his tongue in and out of her moist opening.

Rebecca moaned softly and rocked back and forth against his mouth. All the incendiary delights of that afternoon burst into the flames of raw passion. Searing convulsions ripped through her. She moved her hands to her breasts and squeezed and rolled her hard nipples, all the while frantically grinding her pussy against his hungry mouth. She screamed and whimpered as waves of ecstasy swept through her body.

The door to the bedroom opened, and Elsa

silently crossed the room to the bed. She quickly removed her clothes, climbed onto the bed and straddled Edward's hips. Her pussy was hot and very wet. Rebecca's screams and whimpers fueled Elsa's own needs. She lowered her gaping cunt onto Edward's extremely hard erection.

Edward felt Elsa's pussy muscles grab hold of his cock. She began climaxing as soon as she completely encased him, her convulsions squeezing his prick harder than usual. He had never felt her as hot as she was at that moment.

Rebecca was only vaguely conscious that someone else was on the bed with them. She was so lost in her own rapture that everything else was a blur. She was aware that the new arrival had reached around her, removed her own hands from her breasts and replaced them with their hands. The feel of someone else's hands on her heaving globes excited her even more. She was also aware of Edward's increased lingual attack on her private parts—it was almost as if he had been driven to a new level of intensity.

The only reality Rebecca knew at that moment was what Edward's mouth was doing to her pussy and the stranger's hands were doing to her nipples. Then a new sensation was added, as a pair of soft lips and a tongue kissed, nibbled and licked at the nape of her neck. She ceased to think; she could only delight in each new enchantment.

Edward—his cock tugged mercilessly by Elsa's hungry pussy—erupted, his hot semen shooting into Elsa's cunt for what seemed like several minutes. Rebecca collapsed back against Elsa in a whimpering and quivering heap, her body drained of every ounce of energy. Elsa gasped at the intensity of the moment as the torrid sensations swept through her, generated as much by the feel of Rebecca's firm breasts and hard nipples as by Edward's magnificent cock stretching and filling her and geysering into her cavern.

Elsa's excitement was also fueled by the knowledge that if all went according to schedule, she would now have her turn with Rebecca's body.

SIX

Elsa rolled off Edward, pulling Rebecca with her. All three of them were gasping for breath, trying to regain some sort of composure. Rebecca was, by far, the most out of control, not comprehending exactly what was happening around her or to her—not surprising, considering her lack of experience.

Elsa quickly and efficiently turned Rebecca around and snuggled the girl's trembling body between her own spread legs. She gently but firmly pulled Rebecca's face against her steaming pussy until Edward's hot cream, mixed with her flowing pussy juices, oozed onto Rebecca's mouth.

Rebecca didn't know where she was, who she was with, or what was happening. All she knew was that her body was on fire, that incredibly intense sensations titillated every nerve, and that the same smell and taste Edward had scooped from his rampaging cock and that she had sucked off his finger was at her mouth. Her tongue flicked out, lapping at the moisture. She didn't know where it came from, didn't know what her tongue was touching—and didn't care. She only knew she craved more and more.

Elsa's body stiffened as soon as Rebecca's tongue flicked against her hot cunt. She hadn't expected Rebecca to respond so quickly and so positively. Elsa's clit and love tunnel still tingled from her ride on Edward's cock, making these latest sensations more intense than they would normally have been.

Rebecca sucked and lapped at Elsa's pussy until the taste of Edward's semen was completely dissipated. Only then did she become truly aware of what she was doing. The precise moment she became totally cognizant that she had her mouth against another woman's private place was clearly discernible to both Elsa and Edward.

Edward rested on his haunches at the head of the bed, catching his breath, as he watched Rebecca's beautiful rear end bob and dance in the air. As soon as she showed signs of being aware of what was really going on, he nudged his body up behind her and inserted two fingers into her wet pussy. He wanted to keep her arousal at a high level to distract her.

Rebecca was suddenly horrified and repulsed at the realization that she had her mouth on Elsa's vagina. She was now fully aware that her body nestled between Elsa's legs and that she had actually licked and sucked on another woman's cunt. The full magnitude of her transgression and the repugnance she felt at having performed the sinful act swept through her body. She struggled to pull away from Elsa, but

Edward held her in place, his fingers still embedded in her pussy.

"You can't leave yet, Rebecca. You haven't finished with Elsa, and she hasn't even had an opportunity to make love to you yet. Look at her: do you see how excited you've made her? She wants you to continue satisfying her with your mouth. She also wants to savor the taste of your sweet pussy."

Rebecca felt her stomach churn as she listened to his words. She had performed a vile deed, and now he wanted her to perform it again and to let Elsa perform the same vile act on her. She continued to struggle, wanting desperately to escape from between Elsa's legs.

Edward shot a quick look at Elsa and removed his hand from between Rebecca's legs. He didn't want to take a chance on Rebecca feeling permanently alienated from Elsa before her indoctrination was complete.

Elsa took her cue from Edward and quickly climbed off the bed and silently left the room. A couple of minutes later she entered the security room and stood behind Gunthar, slipping her arms around his shoulders and nibbling at the nape of his neck. "We almost had her. She was so hot and excited, so out of it, that she didn't care what she was doing as long as it continued. When we've finished, she'll be one of our most talented converts."

Gunthar zoomed the camera shot in tight on the bed. "What does Edward have planned for the rest of the evening? I thought we were going to run the videotapes and pipe in the other sound effects, but he's still in bed with her."

"As far as I know, that's still the plan." Both continued to watch the television monitor as Edward attempted to allay Rebecca's fears.

"There's nothing for you to be upset about, Rebecca. Everything that just happened here was very natural." His voice was soothing and soft as he tried to instill in her a sense of well-being and acceptance. "The pleasures of the body aren't limited to only the conventional male on top and female on the bottom as he inserts his penis into her vagina. The variety is endless. You've already experienced the pleasures that a tongue and lips can provide...what difference does it make if that mouth belongs to a man or a woman?"

Rebecca's voice was small and frightened. "It's wrong, that's all. It's just wrong. Maybe what you've forced me to do so far isn't all that bad, but—"

"Forced you to do? Are you really trying to tell me that you haven't enjoyed our activities?" He purposely allowed a hint of amusement to creep into his voice. "Why, Rebecca...your excitement was at such a high level I thought for a moment I might actually drown in the flood of your love juices. You were whimpering, screaming and writhing in such abandoned ecstasy that I was concerned you might pass out from the intense pleasure."

He added the final touch as he tickled his fingers across her inner thigh and tweaked her swollen clit. "If you recall, you even begged me to fuck you—and at the top of your lungs, too." He saw anger flash in her eyes and felt her body stiffen.

She attempted to back away from him, from his sensual touch, from the electric sensations he created deep inside her. He refused to allow her to escape his manipulation of her body. It angered her that it was so maddeningly easy for him, all he had to do was touch her and she immediately submitted.

She loved and craved the unbridled excitement he created in her, but at the same time she hated him for what he was able to do to her and what he was able to make her do. Now he wanted her to do more, to perform abhorrent acts with someone of her own sex. Even though he wasn't laughing at her inexperience, he was still inflicting total humiliation on her. She shuddered at the realization that he could—and would—make her do anything he wanted and she was helpless to resist.

He pushed his finger between the folds of her slit and continued to rub her clit. His breath was hot against her cheek as he whispered his words in a low voice. "Show me how you pleasure yourself, what you do to excite your pussy and make your juices flow. Show me how you achieve your own fulfillment."

With his free hand he grasped hers and moved it between her legs. "Show me how you touch yourself. Do you just rub your clit, insert your finger into your pussy, do both with the same hand, or do you use both hands? Elsa uses both hands. Which do you prefer? Show me, Rebecca. Show me how you do it." He replaced his hand with hers, pushing her finger into her wet cunt and resting her thumb against her clit.

Sounds seemed to be emanating from all around her, coming out of the air: the sounds of people moaning, whimpering, gasping, deep in the throes of wanton sexual pleasures.

Her eyes grew wide as the sounds invaded her senses. She couldn't shut them out, couldn't make them go away. Her heart pounded and her breathing grew ragged. The sounds, seemed to surround her, bombard her from all angles.

The erotic paintings on the walls—they seemed to be alive, seemed to move to the sounds. She tried to focus her attention on what was happening. It wasn't the paintings that were alive. The movement came from another source. The large area of white fabric was now alive with writhing, panting bodies.

She tried not to see or hear, but she couldn't help herself. Each panel depicted a different erotic activity, all taking place in front of her eyes. The sights, the sounds—they overwhelmed her senses. More was happening than she could absorb at one time.

She looked at the orgiastic activity on the walls. Couples were engaged in straight sex. Groups of people were so entangled she couldn't follow who was doing what to whom. Women were engaged in forbidden activities with other women and men were engaged in comparable activities with other men. Female tongues lashed gaping pussies; cocks entered male mouths.

There were close-ups showing a man's jerking tool slipping in and out of a woman's mouth as her hands cradled his balls. Droplets of saliva and sperm glistened on his hard shaft and clung to her lips.

One woman was alone on a bed, her eyes closed, her body writhing from side to side, her knees bent, her heels planted firmly on the mattress, her thighs wide apart and her hand buried in the thick moss adorning her mount. Rebecca's own hand was still where Edward had placed it, tight against her hot pussy.

Rebecca's gaze remained fixed on the image of the woman. She stared, mesmerized, as the woman frantically moved the fingers of her left hand in and out of her wet opening while rubbing and pulling on her clit with her right hand. She could clearly discern the wet pussy fur, the swollen lips and the slick juices on the woman's fingers.

The sounds—the primal noises of heightened sexual arousal—penetrated to the very core of her being. Rebecca's ragged breathing blended with the din. She felt her pussy muscles contract around her fingers, felt the tingling in her clit. Long-buried cravings and desires ran rampant through her body. She began moving her fingers, trying to satisfy the persistent urges. She frantically searched for the spot Edward had so skillfully manipulated.

The torrid waves swept through her. She gasped for air and grabbed at her cunt. She tried to pull on her clit at the same time as she thrust a finger into her slit. She couldn't coordinate both activities using only one hand. Desperate for the orgasm that was building inside her, she quickly shoved her other hand between her legs and thrust her fingers as deeply inside her tunnel as she could.

The sounds permeated the air: the gasping, the moaning, the screaming, the whimpering. She thrust her hips into the air as she finger-fucked her cunt with hard, forceful jabs. The convulsions ripped through her body with lightning speed. She screamed and collapsed back against the soft pillows. Both hands remained firmly entrenched between her legs.

Rebecca's fogged vision slowly cleared. The first and only thing she was able to focus on was her own reflection in the mirrors on the ceiling and the one angled down from the ceiling at the foot of the bed. Her eyes widened in horror at the sight of her damp skin, her open legs and her own hands clutching her swollen pussy and covered with her own slick juices.

Edward quickly threw his arms around her, preventing her from freeing her hands from her pussy. Her body continued to tremble even though her breathing had nearly returned to normal. He took her right nipple into his mouth, running his tongue over the pebbled surface. Watching her writhe seductively while bringing herself to orgasm had him fully aroused. He wanted her again. He ached for her.

The sounds continued—the sounds of sex, the sounds of orgasm, the sounds of wanton lust being thoroughly explored and enjoyed. He took both her hands away from her pussy. He pressed one of them to his mouth, seductively sucking and licking each finger. He pressed the other to her lips. She immediately licked her nectar until her fingers were clean.

The pictures continued to dance across the walls and be reflected in the mirrors. Rebecca's heart pounded in her chest, her blood raced through her veins. Nothing mattered, nothing was important, except having Edward make love to her. She wanted him; she wanted his beautiful cock to stretch and fill her aching cunt.

She was still very wet and very hot. Edward thrust her onto her back and kneed her thighs apart. His hard prick slid easily into her tight tunnel, her pussy muscles grabbing and holding his rigid shaft. His mouth was on hers, his tongue twining with her tongue. Her arms and legs wrapped around his body as her hips moved with his. She was more than simply allowing him to make love to her, she was totally and enthusiastically giving herself to him—relishing each and every delicious sensation that coursed through her body.

Edward wrapped his fingers around her blond tresses and began a slow fucking rhythm. He felt her searing heat as he moved in and out of her, felt her excitement build with each solid thrust. This was what he wanted from her, a totally uninhibited and voluntary response. Next he needed to get the same response from her to new ideas and endeavors.

He gave no more conscious thought to his plans. He immersed himself in the burning desires washing through his body, lost himself in his primal needs. His strokes came harder and faster as he rushed toward orgasm. He pounded his cock into her, his balls slapping her upturned bottom with each stroke.

Rebecca gave up all pretense of objection. She flowed with his movements, melted into the heat of his passion. Never had she imagined that anything connected with sex could be so breathtaking, so magnificent. Never had she imagined that she would want and need Edward Canton's cock embedded in her lusting pussy.

The security room was filled with the sounds of carnal desires—not only the sounds from the speakers, but the added moans and sighs of Elsa and Gunthar. The scent of sex filled the air. Elsa and Gunthar had long ago shed their clothes and were now deeply involved in their own pleasures.

Elsa cradled his balls as she took his cock deep down her throat. Her tongue teased and swabbed; her lips slid up and down his length; her fingers danced along the separation of his ass cheeks, then slowly penetrated his anus. The taste and texture of his cock thrilled her senses.

Gunthar's lips tugged at her pussy fur, nibbled at her inner pussy lips and closed around her engorged clit. His tongue thrust in and out of her opening. His nose, cheeks and chin glistened with a coating of her copious pussy juices. He continued to provide her with what she loved and craved the most.

Elsa continued to suck him frantically, seeking to extract every drop of sperm from his balls. Her lips were wrapped tightly around his tool as she bobbed her head up and down and pumped him with her fist around the base of his shaft.

Gunthar pushed into her, securing his length in her throat, enjoying the way the head of his cock was tickled by her gullet. He tugged on her quivering clit with his teeth, feeling her shudder as he did so. His fingers separated her moss-covered folds to ease the entry of his tongue, anxious to sample more of the juices that already smeared his chin. He lapped up and down, from side to side, in and out. Using his tongue as a miniature penis, he thrust into her channel, establishing a rhythm that soon had Elsa bucking beneath him as her passion overcame her.

Almost an hour passed before Edward silently slipped out of Rebecca's bedroom. He paused at the door and gave one final look back at the sleeping woman, then he returned to her bedside. Her body still glistened with a thin sheen of perspiration; his sperm still trickled from between her swollen pussy lips. He pulled the sheet up to her shoulders and left the suite. He saw no reason to lock her door; he knew she wouldn't try to escape.

She had finally collapsed from exhaustion. He had pushed her to the very limits of her physical and psychological endurance. She wasn't yet experienced enough to know how to pace herself, to have the type of stamina required to withstand the intensity of continual sexual activity.

He entered the security room. Gunthar was shutting down the monitor system. Elsa had already gone to their bedroom. Edward surveyed the scattered clothing, absorbed the heavy aroma of sex. With a slightly bemused expression, he said: "Did you at least manage to record Rebecca's foray into the world of autoeroticism before you abandoned yourself to lust?"

Gunthar placed the last videotape in the safe before replying to Edward's question. "Two angles, in living color and superb graphic detail. Do you want to see it?"

Edward put his hand on Gunthar's shoulder and

gave an affectionate squeeze. "Not tonight. I'm going to get a little sleep. I imagine Rebecca will sleep for several hours. We'll meet before breakfast. I'm returning to Boston tomorrow morning." With that, Edward departed and went straight to his own bedroom.

The morning sun was just coloring the sky when Edward emerged from his bedroom and padded barefoot to the swimming pool. Without hesitation, he executed a perfect dive from the board and began swimming laps up and down the length of the large pool. His form was fluid, his strokes strong, accomplished with measured precision and perfection.

Edward continued his laps for half an hour, then climbed out of the pool. Grabbing a towel, he dried himself off and headed for the dining patio. Elsa and Gunthar sat at the table enjoying their morning coffee and juice. He joined them, pouring himself a cup of coffee. He looked questioningly from Elsa to Gunthar. "Has anyone checked on Rebecca this morning? Is she still sleeping?"

"Gunthar checked the monitor, and I went into her room. She's still totally out of it." Elsa finished the last of the orange juice in her glass. "What's on for today? Gunthar says you're going back to Boston this morning. After her reaction to me last night, I thought you'd be staying another day."

"Can't. I have some pressing business that must be handled in person. I think it's going to be okay. Take it easy with her today, and if you need to, return to the added stimulation of the tapes. Hold off on the Randall Carpenter tape until I get back, in two or three days." He sipped at his coffee, his brow furrowed.

"Gunthar, familiarize her with your touch; get her

accustomed to having your hands on her. Don't be too aggressive about fucking her though; take it slow and easy. She's still easily spooked, but see if you can get her into a threesome by the end of tomorrow—without forcing her."

He turned his attention to Elsa. "Get her to give you free access to her body by the end of today, if possible. Also, see if you can get your finger up her asshole without her becoming hysterical. That should pave the way for Gunthar to penetrate her tomorrow before the threesome tomorrow night. If you can get all that accomplished today and tomorrow, before my return, there'll be a bonus for both of you."

Elsa and Gunthar exchanged quick looks of expectation. It was Elsa who spoke for both of them. "A bonus? What kind of a bonus?"

Edward grinned knowingly. "Money, if that's what you prefer. Or, perhaps I could arrange..." He allowed his voice to trail off as he saw a lascivious glow brighten the eyes of his employees.

He quickly changed the subject. "Elsa, I think you should attend to Rebecca. Gunthar and I are going to get in a couple of sets of tennis before breakfast." All three rose from the table and left the patio.

Elsa entered Rebecca's bedroom and found her still sleeping. After pulling the sheet away from Rebecca's nude body, she climbed into bed with her. Elsa's gaze slowly traveled across the sleeping woman's body, roving over her perfect breasts, slim waist, long legs and tantalizing valley that promised such carnal delight. As had Edward, she found the sparse covering of straight, pale pussy hair very exciting.

Elsa lowered her face between Rebecca's parted legs. Without actually touching the temptingly available pussy, she inhaled the fragrance of Rebecca's scent. Shivers ran up and down her spine as her excitement over what was about to happen made her clit tingle. She reached out and lightly skimmed her fingers over Rebecca's rosy nipples. She delighted as they immediately puckered into taut peaks, just waiting to be suckled.

The sensual touch of Elsa's fingers caused Rebecca to stir awake. At first she was disoriented, then she jerked to attention, sitting bolt upright as she realized Elsa was the one causing the renewed sensations. She started to protest, then Elsa gently cupped the underside of one of her breasts and slowly drew the delicate nipple into the warmth of her mouth. Her touch was soft and light, very different from Edward's touch.

Tremors of pleasure and anticipation darted through Rebecca's body as Elsa continued to suck her tit. With her other hand Elsa teased the other nipple, using the same gentle touch. Rebecca's mind kept telling her this was wrong, terribly wrong, but her body responded to the forbidden treat. Her breathing became ragged as Elsa teased, licked and suckled at her firm breasts.

Elsa's soft touch and sensual mouth very quickly brought Rebecca to arousal. It was so different from the way Edward touched her, but was equally titillating. She reluctantly admitted to herself that Elsa was creating desires in her. She could feel the dampness forming between her legs. She ran her fingertips lightly across Elsa's shoulder, then quickly withdrew her hand.

The sensation of the pebbled texture surrounding Rebecca's hard nipples excited Elsa as she began to explore Rebecca's inviting body. She could tell from Rebecca's increased breathing, her lack of resistance, and the way Rebecca had lightly skimmed her fingertips across her shoulder that the arousal she hoped to create was nearly a reality. The nipple tasted as delicious as it looked, as delicious as she knew it would. She decided to be more daring.

Her fingers tickled Rebecca's inner thighs. She felt the heat radiate from Rebecca's moistening pussy. She gently touched the delicate inner pussy lips, the moisture of Rebecca's excitement seeping from between them. She slowly inserted her finger all the way into the wet opening, worked it around, then withdrew it. While suckling on one nipple Elsa touched her pussy-soaked finger to the other nipple. Then she took the other nipple into her mouth, delighting in the sweet taste.

Rebecca was well on her way to being totally seduced. Her resistance, her objection to what she had been calling "unnatural" was nearly gone. Her body moved in a slow, undulating manner. Her hips thrust slightly upward as her cunt tingled insistently.

Elsa was pleased with the obvious results of her ministrations. Her own clit twitched at the prospect of having Rebecca's mouth buried in her muff. She again inserted her finger into Rebecca's wet pussy, then slowly moved it in and out while circling Rebecca's love button with her thumb.

She wanted Rebecca, wanted her immediately, but knew she couldn't rush her. Edward didn't want her forced and fearful; he wanted to see willingness and enthusiasm. She continued to stimulate Rebecca's clit as she watched her reaction to what was happening to her.

Rebecca's breasts rose and fell. Her pussy was hot and becoming very wet. Elsa saw confusion and wariness in her eyes, but also excitement and desire. She continued her seduction as she spoke in a soothing voice. "There's no reason to be afraid of me,

Rebecca. I'm here to give you pleasure, to share new experiences with you, to teach you to enjoy new delights." She leaned forward and lightly brushed Rebecca's quivering lips, tasting the saltiness of the girl's tears before darting her soft tongue into Rebecca's mouth.

SEVEN

Elsa removed her finger from Rebecca's pussy and touched it to her own lips. She slowly ran her tongue around the finger and licked it clean. She could taste Edward's sperm, still present from the previous night. The taste of Rebecca's honey-sweet nectar delighted her senses. Elsa wanted to bury her mouth in this sweet muff and feast to her heart's content. She would save this treat for a little later, though. Right now it was almost time to join Edward and Gunthar on the dining patio.

Elsa reluctantly removed herself from Rebecca's bed. "Come on, Rebecca. Let's prepare for breakfast and for the events of the day." She guided Rebecca toward the bathroom and turned on the shower. Like

Edward had done the day before, she intended to use the sensually erotic atmosphere of the steamy shower to further her enticement of Rebecca.

Rebecca was only mildly surprised when Elsa entered the shower with her. There was no doubt in her mind that she would be required to allow Elsa to make love to her and she would be expected to reciprocate. She also suspected that before the day was out she would have to submit to Gunthar's sexual attentions. She closed her eyes as the warm spray of the shower settled over her trembling body. She wondered if Edward would ever allow her to return to her home.

Elsa worked the soap into a frothy lather, slowly spread it across Rebecca's shoulders, down her back and onto her bottom. She knelt down behind Rebecca and continued to apply the lather to her legs all the way down to her feet. She rose, trailing her fingers up to Rebecca's rear end.

She cupped Rebecca's firm bottom cheeks and massaged them, working her fingers closer and closer to the separation of those globes. She felt Rebecca's body stiffen when she ran her index finger along the edge of that separation. Without revealing any knowledge of Rebecca's previous hysterical behavior, she smoothly moved her fingers across the width of her hips and then encircled her body.

Elsa spread the soapy lather across the front of Rebecca's thighs, covered her abdomen and stomach, then reached up to take her hands and place them on her breasts, encouraging Rebecca to manipulate and stroke her own nipples. Elsa returned her hands to Rebecca's love nest, rubbing the lather into her mossy patch and across her inner thighs.

Elsa could feel Rebecca tremble when her fingers moved between Rebecca's delicate pussy lips and gently tugged at her hard clit. She kept one hand between Rebecca's legs, manipulating her love button and teasing the folds of her slit. Her other hand moved back to Rebecca's beautiful bottom, again tracing the separation.

She smoothed the soapy lather over Rebecca's buttocks and applied a little more pressure to her clit, becoming more aggressive in her manipulation of Rebecca's tempting love nest. If she could manipulate her to orgasm at the same time as she penetrated her anus with a finger, Rebecca would be absorbed by the pleasure rather than whatever it was that had created the hysterical response to Edward's having touched her.

Rebecca's breasts rose and fell with her erratic breathing. Elsa's touch was so light and gentle, and so very sensual. It seemed to merge with the warm spray and the sudsy lather that cascaded over her body. She tried to tell herself that what was happening to her was depraved and perverted, that although she couldn't prevent it from happening, she certainly didn't need to participate in it.

The only problem with her thoughts was that they failed to stop the sensations that swept through her body. Her legs trembled. She reached out and placed her hand against the shower wall in an effort to steady herself.

Elsa felt Rebecca's heightened excitement, quickly assessed each and every sign of her arousal. She maneuvered herself around until she faced Rebecca, never letting up on her stimulation of Rebecca's engorged clit. Her own breathing became ragged as she watched the rivulets of water wash the lather from Rebecca's breasts, droplets clinging to her hard nipples. She bent her head forward and took one of the tempting peaks into her mouth.

Rebecca shivered as Elsa's mouth closed over her excited nipple. Rather than sucking on it, Elsa held it in the warmth of her mouth, softly teasing it with her tongue. Rebecca didn't know what to do or how to respond. She sincerely believed that what Elsa was doing to her was very wrong, very sinful; yet, it felt so exciting and wonderful. The sensations made her body come alive with delight.

Elsa continued to tease and massage Rebecca's love button with one hand while she deftly trailed her fingers through the sudsy lather that covered her bottom. Each foray moved Elsa's fingers closer and closer to Rebecca's anus, closer and closer to penetrating the soap-lubricated opening.

Rebecca's heart pounded and her pulse raced. The warm spray washed over her breasts and trickled down to her feet. The steam swirling around her head lent everything a dreamlike aura. The moist air filled her lungs as her breathing became labored. Her entire body tingled with the forbidden excitement of Elsa's touch. She could feel her pussy muscles grabbing at Elsa's fingers.

In the back of her mind she was vaguely aware of the nearness of Elsa's fingers to the last place she would ever permit anyone to touch her. Elsa's sensual seduction temporarily blocked the horrifying memories from her mind. Rebecca relaxed and allowed her body to flow with the feelings.

Elsa kept Rebecca's body at a level of excitement just short of orgasm. She slipped two fingers inside Rebecca's love tunnel while she continued to titillate Rebecca's clit with her thumb. She could feel the pussy muscles contracting, hear Rebecca's moans and whimpers. Slowly, ever so slowly, she slipped a soapy finger into Rebecca's rosebud opening and held it there. She felt Rebecca's muscles immediately tense and her body stiffen. She maintained a strong grip, refusing to allow her to pull away.

The shock of feeling something enter her anus, even though the penetration was smooth and not painful, sent waves of fear through Rebecca's mind. Nothing mattered except getting away from this most horrible of violations. But she found Elsa's surprising strength too much for her. She was unable to pull away or dislodge Elsa's finger from her bottom. Her moans and whimpers quickly turned to cries of fear and panic.

Elsa talked to Rebecca as she held the frightened woman motionless in the shower. As her words calmed Rebecca's panic, her fingers continued to manipulate her pussy and gently stimulate her anus. "Relax, Rebecca. There's nothing to be frightened of. I'm not going to hurt you, I'm only going to show you more ways to enjoy the pleasures of the body. Feel the sensations flowing through your sweet pussy, the way they now extend to your bottom. I can feel it, Rebecca. This finger," she wiggled the finger embedded in Rebecca's cunt, "can actually sense what this finger," for the first time she moved the finger in the rosebud opening, "is doing."

Rebecca's sobs softened. Elsa continued to talk to her in a soothing voice. "What is it that frightens you so? I know your bottom isn't virgin. I can tell by looking that it's been penetrated before, more than once. Relax your muscles, you're much too tense. Since you've already been introduced to the pleasures of anal intercourse, why are you so reticent? I really don't understand, Rebecca. Tell me."

Elsa's words floated across Rebecca's consciousness. Rebecca felt her own panic beginning to subside, her tension beginning to drain away. Elsa's touch was gentle and soft. Even with the sudden blanket of panic enveloping her, the primal urges coursing through her muff never really subsided. Rebecca was so confused about everything. Elsa's penetration of her anus, she begrudgingly admitted to herself, was neither painful nor humiliating.

Elsa continued her gentle stimulation, moving her finger back and forth. "Tell me, Rebecca. Tell me what happened to make you so frightened."

Rebecca could hold back her inner turmoil no longer; she burst into tears. She stood in the shower, her entire body trembling. She had never told anyone what had happened. But suddenly it seemed all right if she told Elsa. She wanted to tell someone, to set the demons free.

Elsa sensed the breakthrough. She knew Rebecca needed comfort at this moment rather than sexual stimulation. She put her arms around the sobbing girl's shoulders and held her. "Tell me, Rebecca. Let go of whatever it is."

She maneuvered Rebecca from the shower, wrapped a large towel around her and led her into the bedroom. Rebecca offered no resistance as Elsa positioned her on her stomach in the middle of the large bed and removed the towel from around her body. "Tell me, Rebecca."

Elsa uncapped a bottle of massage oil and poured some on Rebecca's back. With firm strokes she worked the oil over the girl's skin, kneading away the tension in her muscles. She felt Rebecca relax as she worked her fingers across her shoulders, down her arms, across her back—finally arriving at Rebecca's pert bottom.

Elsa gave special care and attention to Rebecca's beautiful ass. She massaged, squeezed and kneaded the tantalizing flesh, working her fingers up and down the separation of her firm cheeks. She felt

Rebecca flinch as she touched her bottomhole again, but this time Rebecca didn't try to pull away. She slowly slipped her oily finger into the puckered opening.

"See, Rebecca? There's nothing here to be frightened about. Can you feel the delicious sensation of my finger moving in and out? Isn't it exciting? I don't understand why this delightful activity should frighten you."

"This...this isn't too bad." Rebecca's words were tentative, unsure. She found the sensations oddly pleasurable. "It's very different from..." Her words trailed off. She was having difficulty finishing her sentence.

"Different from what?" Elsa spoke calmly, conveying a warm feeling of trust and confidence. She continued to gently thrust her finger in and out of Rebecca's anus.

"From when..." Rebecca wanted to tell someone what had happened, the cruelty and humiliation she had been forced to endure. She closed her eyes and took a deep breath. The words gushed out in a torrent.

"Jason raped me on a date. I was a virgin. When he had finished with me, he laughed and said I was a lousy lay. That was the last time I saw him until I found out I was pregnant. My parents paid him to marry me. On our wedding night he told me my...uh..." Rebecca was having difficulty repeating the words Jason had used, "...my cunt had been boring and maybe my ass would be more to his liking.

"He pinned me down on the bed and rammed his penis up my bottom. It was the most excruciating pain I've ever felt. He wouldn't stop, he just kept doing it until he was satisfied. Then, when his discharge seeped out of me, and I saw it was mixed with blood, I became so very frightened. I didn't know what he'd done to me. It felt and looked as though he'd torn my insides apart. He did the same thing to me five more times in the next two days, each time more horrible than the one before. Instead of it becoming easier, it became more painful. He would grab me by the hair or by my breasts from behind and ride me like I was an animal. And all the time he kept pounding into my anus. I don't know why he decided to finally leave me alone and take his sexual perversions elsewhere."

Rebecca's entire body trembled as years of pent up emotions finally relinquished their hold on her. Sobs wracked her body. It was finally out in the open, someone else knew the torture she had endured.

Edward and Gunthar stood in the security room, intently watching and listening to everything. Edward let out a low whistle. "Well, that certainly explains a lot."

Gunthar's face was an expressionless mask as he turned to Edward. "It's almost unbelievable that you've gotten this far with her this quickly considering what had to be overcome."

Edward's brow was furrowed. "Sex is for pleasure. It shouldn't be for pain unless pain is what gives you pleasure." His eyes darkened as he stared intently at Gunthar. "Perhaps we should do something about this Jason—just on principle."

Gunthar raised an eyebrow and cocked his head to one side. "Perhaps so."

Both men returned their attention to the monitor.

Elsa had moved from her position behind Rebecca and was now comforting the nearly hysterical woman. Even though Rebecca was four inches taller than Elsa, she seemed much smaller as Elsa cradled her in her arms and gently rocked her.

Elsa shifted her position so that Rebecca's mouth was in close proximity to her breast. She continued to comfort Rebecca. "Go ahead and cry, dear. Get it out of your system. Now that you've let go of it things will be okay." With one arm still around Rebecca's shoulder, she cupped the underside of her own breast and offered it to Rebecca's lips.

Rebecca's painful catharsis had resulted in a need for contact and comfort, the closeness of a caring person. When Elsa touched her breast to Rebecca's lips, Rebecca took the nipple into her mouth and began to suck gently—almost like a baby suckling at its mother's breast. The sensation filled her with a sense of calm.

Elsa closed her eyes, allowing the sensations elicited by Rebecca's soft mouth to flow over her. She tickled her fingers across Rebecca's mount, then inserted two fingers into her love nest. She felt Rebecca's immediate response to the stimulation in her increased fervor.

Rebecca moaned softly, losing herself in the hitherto unknown sensation of having a woman's nipple in her mouth. She was aware of Elsa's fingers tickling her pussy lips and penetrating her love nest. She was also aware that Elsa had gently stretched her out on the bed, was no longer cradling her body. Elsa slowly but methodically maneuvered Rebecca into the desired position. She carefully withdrew her nipple from Rebecca's mouth and turned around so that her mouth was at Rebecca's sweet pussy.

Rebecca shivered as Elsa's tongue flicked so close to her private place. The sensations aroused delicious tremors deep inside her. Her hands went to her own breasts, massaging her erect nipples until they ached. How could something so sinful be so exciting at the same time? She gave up trying to rationalize it.

Elsa lowered her pussy to Rebecca's mouth, placing it only a tongue's flick away. Rebecca instinctively took Elsa's engorged clit into her mouth and sucked like she had with Edward's finger. The texture, the shape, the folds, the scent—everything about this forbidden act excited her. Elsa's flowing pussy juices filled her mouth with a tantalizing new taste. She eagerly drank it down as she continued to lap at the delectable treat.

Elsa's moans and screams titillated Rebecca's senses, spurring on her actions. It was wrong, so very wrong, but she couldn't stop herself. She eagerly devoured this new taste and sensation.

Rebecca's quivering pussy was soon enjoying the expert ministrations of Elsa's talented mouth. Elsa's tongue teased the delicate pussy lips as she circled the entrance to Rebecca's love tunnel. Her lips gently tugged at Rebecca's fur, then nibbled at her sensitive clit. She darted her tongue at the fleshy peak, pleased at the tremors her ministrations elicited from Rebecca. Then she began to lick the folds of her pussy with long, wet strokes that had Rebecca writhing beneath her and whimpering, begging her for more.

Eager to comply, Elsa drilled into Rebecca's slit, burying her tongue as far as she could and lashing it from side to side. Her fingers opened the moist tunnel even wider so that she could delve more deeply into its recesses. Her thumb continued to work on Rebecca's clit, circling it, flicking it, teasing it until it stood red and swollen.

After subjecting Rebecca to prolonged pleasure, Elsa finally took her clit fully into her mouth and began a sensual sucking motion. At the same time she again inserted her finger into Rebecca's anus.

Rebecca erupted in an intense orgasm. She thrust

her hips sharply upward, forcing her cunt hard against Elsa's mouth. At the same time, she wrapped her arms around Elsa's hips and buried her tongue deep inside Elsa's pussy.

Elsa had been holding back on her own release. She wanted Rebecca to experience orgasm with a woman before she indulged in her own pleasures. But now, the sight and sound of Rebecca experiencing orgasm pushed Elsa over the edge to her own rapture, and she released a copious amount of her pearly nectar into Rebecca's mouth.

Both women remained still, trying to bring their breathing back to normal. Rebecca tried to straighten out in her mind what had just happened. She had experienced deliciously intense waves of ecstasy, an ecstasy stimulated by another woman. It had been every bit as exciting as anything Edward had created in her.

Elsa was the first to move. She placed a soft kiss on each of Rebecca's nipples. Then she rose and stood next to the bed. "Come on, we need to get ready for breakfast." She paused as she allowed her gaze to drift over Rebecca's beautiful body. "Of course, I can't imagine breakfast even comparing with the delicious taste of your sweet pussy." Elsa smiled inwardly as Rebecca blushed a pretty pink and averted her eyes.

Edward and Gunthar were enjoying a cup of coffee when Rebecca and Elsa finally joined them on the dining patio. The blush of embarrassment lingered on Rebecca's cheeks as they took their places at the table. Gunthar was the first to speak. "You look particularly radiant this morning, Rebecca. Did you have a good night's sleep?"

Rebecca glanced at Gunthar but was unable to hold his gaze. She looked down and answered in a very soft voice. "I slept fine, thank you." She didn't know how he knew, but she was sure that he did—he and Edward both knew what had just happened in her bedroom. She also knew that the three people seated at the table with her found nothing unusual or untoward about what she had just experienced, but that still didn't lessen her embarrassment.

Breakfast proceeded in a casual, upbeat manner. Everyone seemed in good spirits, and even Rebecca began to relax after a little while. The sunlight and balmy tropical breeze played across her skin, warmed her face and arms. She leaned back in her chair, closed her eyes and allowed the bounties of nature to caress her body. For the first time she realized how pale her skin really was. She had already made a mental note of the stark contrast between her skin and Edward's, but the same contrast existed with Elsa and Gunthar, too.

Things were so strange. She had been kidnapped, taken to an isolated tropical island, ensconced in a luxury villa with all the comforts of a deluxe resort, then forced to submit to any number of sexual depravities. Yet here she sat enjoying the sun's rays, basking in the tropical breezes, sharing breakfast with the very people responsible for her captivity and, in general, feeling pretty much at peace with the world.

She no longer felt the terror and panic that had so consumed her that first night and following day. It was almost a relief to not have to put up a facade, to not be required to continue living the lie of wealth and position.

She wondered what would happen to her. Even if Edward did allow her to return to Boston, she couldn't imagine what her life be like. She knew one thing: she could never go back to the type of lifestyle that had relegated her to an empty bed. The door Edward had forced open could never again be closed.

Rebecca came to attention as a hand squeezed her shoulder. She didn't know how long she had been lost in her own thoughts, but when she opened her eyes Elsa and Gunthar were gone. She looked up at Edward standing over her, his body silhouetted against the sun. She shaded her eyes with her hand.

"You shouldn't be in this sun without some lotion to protect your skin. You're inviting a painful sunburn. Your skin is so fair to begin with—it's obvious you never spend any time outdoors. That's too bad."

"I was just thinking how relaxing the sun felt, but you're probably right about sunburn."

He held out his hand to her. "Come on, let's find you some suntan lotion."

Rebecca accepted his hand, rose from her chair and followed him into the house. Edward quickly located a bottle of lotion, then escorted her to the private patio off her bedroom. Without further conversation, he undressed her and positioned her on her back on the chaise longue. He quickly removed his own clothes, never taking his eyes off her alluring form.

She made no effort to hide her nakedness from him and showed no signs of embarrassment at his close scrutiny of her body. She had become comfortable with his presence. She wondered what would happen when it was Gunthar standing over her rather than Edward.

She couldn't help herself as she allowed her gaze to slowly travel over his well-toned body. He was tanned all over with only a hint of a line from a bathing suit, and a very skimpy bathing suit at that. There was no doubt in her mind: Edward Canton was

131

even better looking without clothes than he was dressed.

Edward rested on his knees as he straddled her hips. With very slow, deliberate motions he poured a generous amount of the lotion into his hand. He applied it to her body starting across her neck, continuing over her shoulders, down her arms and returning to her breasts. His hands cupped her luscious mounds as he slowly massaged the oil into the firm flesh, paying particular attention to her hardened nipples.

With obvious reluctance, he left her breasts and continued down her stomach and over her abdomen. His hands spread out, applying the lotion to her hips and up her rib cage before returning to her breasts. His fingers plucked at her nipples, gently tugging on the taut peaks before continuing to massage.

Rebecca's lotion-covered body glistened in the bright sunlight, her rosy nipples standing erect. Her breathing had noticeably quickened, the swell of her breasts rising and falling with each breath. Edward's tone was soft, his voice lulling her. "You have the most exquisitely beautiful body I've ever seen. How is it possible for you to have denied yourself its pleasures all these years?"

Without further comment, he poured more lotion into his hands and applied it to her legs. Kneeling beside her, he worked his fingers along her feet, over her ankles and up her calves to her thighs. He skillfully kneaded her flesh, gradually moving closer and closer to the object of his desire nestled between her thighs.

The now-recognizable signs of her sexual arousal coursed through Rebecca's body. His touch was so sensual, so intimate, so overwhelming—it almost took her breath away. He was right, even though she would never tell him so; how could she have denied herself this ecstasy all these years? If only she had known what it could really be like.

Every place he touched her caused tremors of excitement. She wanted him inside her, wanted the feel of his hard cock completely filling her. She arched her hips toward his hands, the hands that teased the edges of her pussy without actually touching it. She wanted Edward Canton, in every sense of the word and in every possible way. She knew, no matter how much she wanted to deny it, that she would willingly do anything and everything he wanted her to do, would comply with any and all of his needs no matter how depraved she found them. Everything he had said on the plane had come to pass.

Edward was very pleased. He saw the fires of passion in her eyes just as he had prophesied. He saw her hips arch toward him, felt the sensual urgency in her body. She was more than merely allowing him to have his way with her; she wanted what was about to happen. The flames of her desire were running rampant. His fingers lightly traced her pussy lips. His voice was slightly husky as he said: "What do you want, Rebecca? Tell me what you want."

She took a deep breath as she looked into the smoldering charcoal of his eyes. There was no use in pretending or playing games. They both knew what she wanted. She didn't look away as she said the words. "I want you, Edward. I want you to fill me with your cock. I want you to make love to me."

There was no need to prolong the verbal jousting. She had said what he wanted to hear. He covered her entire love nest with the palm of his hand, then slowly slipped one finger into her slit and into the heated core of her body. "No man in his right mind could

133

possibly deny you." He brought his mouth down against hers, capturing her very breath. His tongue twined with hers.

Her arms slipped around his neck; her fingers trailed through his thick hair. She matched his heated intensity as she gave herself to him. Suddenly everything seemed so natural. She functioned from instinct and desire, not waiting for his instructions. She reached for his erect organ, wrapping her fingers sensually around the hard shaft. She gently pumped, her rhythm matching his manipulation of her engorged clit.

Her touch was neither tentative nor uncertain—it was the confident touch of an experienced woman. Edward marveled at the transformation from frigid, unfeeling mannequin to sensual, responsive woman. She was actually throwing her entire being into this. Her body responded honestly and fully to his every move.

He parted her thighs and positioned himself between them, his hard cock probing at her wet opening. She was hot, so very hot. He penetrated her slowly, very slowly, savoring each and every inch of the way into her tunnel. She was incredibly tight. He paused when his cock was completely buried inside her pussy. When he collected his composure, he commenced moving his pole in and out of her box.

Rebecca gasped as he pumped her. She thrust her hips hard against him, trying to take him more deeply into her—if that were possible. His mouth found hers, his tongue penetrating her as surely as his stiff rod penetrated her love tunnel.

He plunged into her with deep, deliberate strokes that thoroughly stretched and filled her pussy. He felt her muscles grab at him with each forward thrust. She became more aggressive, urging him on to a faster rhythm as her tongue fluttered in his mouth. She seemed almost out of control, her very being enveloped by wanton abandon. She seemed to be functioning solely for the purpose of experiencing intense sexual pleasure.

Edward increased his tempo, giving her the added sensual stimulation she seemed to crave. She was out of control, lost in the primal need for unbridled sex. Her legs wrapped tightly around his waist, her hips thrust in the air to meet his every stroke, her arms encircled his strong shoulders and her mouth tasted more and more of him.

Suddenly Edward rolled onto his back, his cock still buried to the hilt in Rebecca's muff. While she reeled in shock, he put his hands on her hips and began moving her up and down on his shaft. He began slowly, only jiggling her, letting her feel the effect of her weight on their fucking. Then he raised her up more and more and let her drop down on his full length until she rode his prick from top to bottom, her eyelids fluttering, her chest heaving from the exquisite agony.

Rebecca screamed out as the intensity of her orgasm swept through her body. As if this were a call to action, Edward thrust harder and harder until his cock pistoned in and out of her faster than seemed humanly possible. He wanted to fuck all of her, every square inch of her body. She cried out again and again as orgasm after orgasm roared through her.

Edward could hold off no longer. He felt his rapture churning in his balls, boiling toward release. He enfolded her tightly in his arms as he gave one final hard thrust. His hot cream shot into her in powerful spurts.

She clung to him, feeling drained but at the same time wanting more and more of him. She couldn't describe the feeling, didn't understand it. Her entire body tingled, and her insides convulsed. She didn't know what she wanted; she only knew that Edward Canton was the answer.

Edward was running behind schedule. He hadn't planned on the delay caused by Elsa's seduction of Rebecca before breakfast. The timing, however, had apparently been right and Elsa had proceeded. He should have been in the air headed back for Boston. The change in Rebecca was miraculous—from "Ice Maiden" to hot lover. She was progressing nicely.

Edward rose to his feet and looked at her for a moment longer. "Why don't you stay out for a while, get a little sun—see if you can't get some color. A nice tan will be very striking with your blond hair and blue eyes." He picked up the lotion bottle and poured more into his hands. "Turn over, I'll put some lotion on your back."

He made no sexual forays. After rubbing in the lotion he simply put the cap back on the bottle and gave her one last look before leaving. "I'm flying to Boston as soon as I'm dressed. I should be back in a couple of days. I'm sure Elsa and Gunthar will keep you entertained until I return."

Rebecca was stunned by his announcement and the casual way he presented it. She felt a lump form in the pit of her stomach and a nervous anxiety dart through her body. She wasn't sure what to make of this sudden turn of events. For some odd, unexplainable reason she felt as if she had been abandoned.

His touch excited her, his taste and smell sent a thrill through her. Now he was gone, leaving her to cope with whatever Elsa and Gunthar would demand of her. She closed her eyes and let the warming rays of the sun wash over her oiled body. She soon drifted off into an uneasy sleep.

Rebecca wasn't sure how long she had been asleep. She gradually became aware of someone shaking her shoulder. Her next bit of reality was Gunthar's voice. "You've been on your stomach too long. You need to turn over before you burn." She felt his strong hands roll her over onto her back. It was the first time Gunthar had ever touched her.

She was still nude, hadn't bothered to dress after Edward left. She was stretched out on the chaise longue, with Gunthar looming over her. Anxiety coursed through her as she tried to cover her nakedness with her hands. Even though the sun was warm, she began to shiver.

He pulled her hands away from her body, clasped her wrists together in his firm grip and stretched her arms above her head. He ran his index finger from the notch at the base of her throat straight down her body, between her breasts, ending up in her mossy patch just short of her clit. She tried to pull away from his unsettling touch, to roll her body over and out of his sight, but he wouldn't allow it. He pinned her motionless against the chaise.

"Don't play games with me, Rebecca. Edward was very easy on you. He has a personal interest in all of this—I don't. To me this is a routine job, nothing more."

In an almost indifferent manner he inserted his finger between her pussy lips as she cowered, trying to shrink away from his touch. He stroked her clit with his thumb and immediately felt her juices start to flow. With the same indifference, he withdrew his finger and sucked her taste into his mouth. He released her wrists so that she could lower her arms. His demeanor softened. He smiled as he spoke. "Elsa is right, you do taste very good."

She felt the heat spread across her face and down

her neck. She wasn't sure if she was blushing or if the sun was becoming too hot. She was very aware of his bright, hazel eyes taking in every inch of her nude body. His gaze lingered on her breasts and on her pussy. She moved her hands to cover herself again.

He abruptly changed the mood. "You need some more lotion or you'll burn for sure." He uncapped the lotion bottle, poured some into his hand and began to massage it into her shoulders.

She reached out to take the lotion bottle from him. "I…I can do that myself. In fact, I think I'll get out of the sun…" she moved to get off the lounger, "…and get dressed." She was very nervous, uncomfortable with Gunthar's hands on her bare skin. She had become accustomed to Edward's touch, and thrilled to his lovemaking. Gunthar was different— he wasn't Edward.

Gunthar refused to allow her to leave. His voice was stern without being too harsh. "Don't make me tell you again. I have a job to do, certain things that must be accomplished in a specific time frame. We can do it the easy way, or we can do it the hard way—either way, it will get done. Now relax," he flashed her a smile, "and enjoy." He started at her shoulders and quickly moved to her breasts.

Rebecca was unable to force herself to remain still under his touch. She squirmed as panic welled up inside her. Was this going to be it? Was he going to have his way with her right here and now? She didn't understand why it was necessary for her to be intimate with Gunthar. She had enjoyed everything Edward had done to her. Why did everyone feel it was necessary for her to have sex with Gunthar as well?

She saw momentary anger flash through his hazel eyes as he grabbed her wrist in a firm grip. His voice had a hard edge. "Edward doesn't want you marked or bruised, but if that's the only way to do this then he'll understand. Don't make me force you."

He released her wrist and resumed his massage of the lotion into her skin. His talented fingers kneaded her firm flesh—her shoulders, her arms and finally her breasts. Her nipples hardened into peaks even though she felt far from sexually aroused. Up until now, she had found no reason to be concerned about Gunthar. Now he frightened her.

She tried to disassociate his words from his touch. If she could just enjoy the sensations the way she did with Edward, then maybe things would be all right. She had finally become comfortable with Edward; her fears of him were gone. Now she must start all over again with someone new. She closed her eyes, a tremor starting in the pit of her stomach as he continued to massage her flesh.

His hands moved down her body, smoothing the lotion over her skin. He covered her stomach, her abdomen, and then, without pausing, went immediately to her thighs. He massaged the lotion into her legs and moved his hands toward her inviting pussy.

His touch became more sensual as his fingers danced all around her love box without touching it. As abruptly as it all began, he ceased his ministrations. He studied her for a moment. "Don't stay in the sun for more than a couple of hours. Remain the way you are; your back side has had all the sun it can handle for today." With that, he left the patio, leaving Rebecca stunned and alone.

EIGHT

Elsa and Gunthar stared intently at the monitor in the security room. Rebecca was still on her back on the chaise longue, but she hadn't been quietly sunning herself. She was restless, constantly repositioning herself, trying to get comfortable. Several times she had placed her hands on her body and smoothed the oily lotion around; the last time she had massaged her breasts, her fingers lingering and tugging at her hard nipples. Her legs spread wider apart with each restless move.

She was unhappy with the nervousness that coursed through her. Gunthar's words lingered in her head: *Edward doesn't want you marked or bruised, but if that's the only way to do this then he'll under-*

141

stand. Don't make me force you. There was no doubt
in her mind that he wouldn't hesitate to do something
to her, something violent and painful. The thoughts
frightened her.

Gunthar put his hand on Elsa's shoulder. "It looks
like she's about to take a positive step forward, initiate something on her own. I think she'll have her fingers buried inside that delightful little cunt in less
than five minutes."

"Do you think you went too far, darling, threatening her like that? She's come along so nicely, progressed so much. I'd hate to see her take a step backward because she's afraid that you're going to hurt
her."

"I'm not interested in hurting her," he shot Elsa a
quick grin and a devilish look, "at least not under
these circumstances. But I do insist on her full cooperation. If not..." He allowed his voice to trail off as
they continued to watch Rebecca.

Rebecca smoothed the lotion over her upper legs,
tentatively darting her hands to her inner thighs, then
quickly removing them. She ran her fingers along the
crease where her thighs joined her torso. On her
third excursion along this route her fingers strayed to
her muff and to her outer pussy lips.

She paused as if uncertain about whether to proceed. Then slowly, she allowed her fingers to dance
across her slit and touch her delicate inner pussy lips.
Her breasts rose and fell; her nipples stood hard and
erect.

Gunthar adjusted the camera for a closer look. He
wanted to capture the details of her masturbation but
didn't want to lose the changing shadows of emotion
that crossed her face.

Rebecca's tongue flicked excitedly across her
lips. Her eyes remained closed. She finally inserted

a finger between her pussy lips and into her love tunnel. A little smile of pleasure curled the corners of her mouth as she moved her finger in and out of her wet opening. She softly brushed her clit with her thumb. Her reaction to the torrid sensation that shot through her body was immediate. She shoved her finger deep inside her cunt and vigorously stroked her love button.

Her face clearly registered the sensual pleasures she was giving herself, the depth of her excitement as her body writhed about on the chaise longue.

Gunthar adjusted the camera for an extreme close-up of Rebecca's pussy. Her fingers were covered with her glistening juices as she feverishly worked them in and out of her opening and against her clit.

Her manipulations became erratic and jerky, and her breasts rose and fell with her labored breathing as she pushed hard for the final rapture. She was totally lost in the incendiary sensations she had created in her own body. Everything kept building, layer upon layer, until she was almost beside herself with her need to reach the ultimate plateau. Her head thrashed from side to side, she gasped for air.

Her body stiffened as she was consumed by wave after wave of convulsions. Her pussy juices flowed over her fingers and mingled with the suntan lotion that coated her inner thighs. Tears welled in her eyes and slid down her cheeks as the magnitude of her euphoria settled over her.

She remained still, her fingers embedded between her pussy lips and her thumb resting against her swollen clit. After a few minutes she slowly withdrew her hand. Without hesitation, she put her fingers to her mouth and licked them clean. With a satisfied expression on her beautiful face, she settled back and enjoyed the warm rays of the sun.

"Oh, yes." Gunthar readjusted the camera angle to take in the entire patio. "She's coming along very nicely." He turned toward Elsa and gave her a quick kiss on the cheek. "I don't think there will be any problem with our being able to collect that bonus from Edward. The only question is whether or not he'll be able to deliver that little treat we discussed."

Elsa's eyes glowed with excitement. "Oh, darling. Wouldn't that be just too marvelous? Identical twin girls, not a day over twenty-one, and both virgins—those firm little breasts, lithe bodies and untouched cunts. And just think, they would be all ours and ours alone, to do with as we pleased for as long as we pleased." Her nipples had hardened to peaks, pushing against her tank top.

Gunthar knelt on the floor, tugged at Elsa's shorts and pulled them down to her ankles. "Just a little between-meal snack, Elsa. Then I must attend to Rebecca. If we're going to earn that bonus, she has to willingly accept my prick up her ass before the end of today." He thrust his tongue into Elsa's bush, licked her pussy lips, then closed his mouth over her clit. He tugged on the hot nub of flesh, fascinated as always by the way it quivered when he took it between his teeth. He slid his index finger into her slit at the same time, working it around and stretching her so that in a moment, when he replaced his finger with his tongue, her juices would already be flowing.

As Elsa started to buck her hips from his continued teasing of her love button, he quickly moved his mouth to her tunnel, licking all around the outer folds. He used his fingers to turn back the skin, exposing the pink fleshiness of her inner membranes, and began lapping at it. He varied his strokes by penetrating her passage from time to time, delving into her as far as he could and sending her into paroxysms of delight. Her hands were on the back of his head, urging him on, begging him wordlessly to fuck her again and again with his tongue until it seemed as though her entire body must come apart from the spasms that shook it.

The warming rays of the sun, combined with the totally relaxed state of Rebecca's body and mind, caused her to drift off into a blissful sleep following her self-stimulation. She didn't know how long she had been napping when she, again, became aware of Gunthar's presence. She raised her hand to her eyes to shade them from the bright sun. Her entire body jerked to attention at the sight of Gunthar standing over her, completely naked. His large cock bobbed stiffly in front of him, the head thick and dark. A nervous anxiety coursed through her veins and settled in the pit of her stomach.

She made a quick survey of his physical attributes, unable to curb her curiosity. His body was hard, muscular without being muscle-bound, and tanned all over. He wasn't handsome like Edward but certainly very attractive. His organ, though probably larger than average, didn't measure up to Edward's beautiful penis—not just in size, but also in shape and definition.

She felt the flush of embarrassment cover her cheeks as she realized what she was doing. She unconsciously moved her hands to cover her nakedness. Was this the way it was going to be from now on? Every man in the world would be compared to Edward and found physically lacking?

Gunthar knew that look. He had seen it many times before when he had been involved in Edward's various sexual escapades. A less secure man would have been resentful and jealous; Gunthar was neither. "Comparisons are natural, Rebecca, especially when dealing with Edward. Don't be embarrassed by your thoughts." He saw the silent, grateful "thank you" in her eyes for his immediate understanding of the situation and his acceptance of it as a normal occurrence.

Earlier she had felt fear and anxiety at Gunthar's presence and his words—actually they were threats. Right now, as she surveyed his physical being, she found Gunthar to be a very attractive man who possessed a very charming manner. The two different perspectives resulted in an inner conflict that confused her.

He continued in a calm tone of voice. As he spoke he situated himself next to her. "Everyone makes comparisons." He gently but firmly moved her hands out of the way and played his fingertips across the swell of one breast. He circled her hardening nipple and cupped the entire breast, allowing her taut peak to press into the palm of his hand. He felt her tremble under his touch, felt her body tense, saw her look of apprehension, anxiety and wariness.

He refused to acknowledge the silent fears conveyed by her eyes and her body language. He continued as if she had exhibited no concerns of any kind. "Take you and Elsa, for instance." He forced her tensed legs apart with his knee, then sandwiched his body between her thighs with her pussy resting against his stomach. "Her pussy fur is long and curly and covers just everything. Even after all these years I still get a hard-on just looking at it."

Supporting his upper body on his elbows, he took his other hand and teased her other nipple to a hard peak. "Your pussy, on the other hand, is covered by a fine down. At first glance, one would almost think you had shaved your pussy clean. I find that very exciting too."

Rebecca was being lulled by his smooth tone of voice and his manipulation of her breasts. She felt some of the tension drain away. He had just been very understanding, actually seemed sympathetic to her anxieties.

His tongue flicked out, licking the underside of her breasts and teasing the puckered flesh surrounding her hard nipples. He drew one of the peaks into his mouth and nipped at it with his teeth, then eagerly sucked on the delicious bud. He moved to her other breast, managing a few words before capturing her puckered flesh. "You have perfect tits: perfect to nibble, perfect to suck."

Rebecca felt awkward and uncomfortable about what he was doing to her. Somehow it seemed wrong. For some bizarre reason she felt she was being unfaithful to Edward. She knew she was expected to willingly give herself to Gunthar, that Edward had instructed Gunthar to do these things to her. She also knew she would comply—if for no other reason than Gunthar's deliberate threats to hurt her.

The sensations were building in her again. It didn't seem to matter who caused them—Edward, Gunthar, Elsa, or even she, herself—as long as she could experience them fully and completely. She briefly questioned whether she had turned depraved. She decided it didn't matter.

Gunthar was somewhat surprised by her quick change of attitude and willing response to his stimulation. He hadn't expected her to react that fast to one verbal threat. He hadn't really though there would be any difficulty with her, but he also hadn't anticipated that she would be so spontaneous. He felt the dampness of her pussy shoved against his stomach. Then came the soft touch of her hands skimming across his shoulders, her fingers running through his hair.

His normal technique was to remain emotionally detached and indifferent when involved with one of Edward's "business dealings." This, he could already tell, was going to be different. Years of repression were peeling away from her. She was so hot and so ready. It was going to be very difficult for him to remain indifferent and merely go through the mechanics required to accomplish the job.

Rebecca moaned as her hips thrust hard against his body. He was caught up in her ecstasy, caught up in her earthy arousal. He knew this was going to be more than just a business fuck, sex for the sake of sex. He felt her heat, felt her passion.

Gunthar wanted his throbbing cock buried deep in her hot, wet cunt. Business be damned—he wanted to fuck her long and hard. He needed to show her how defenseless and vulnerable she was, how important it was for her to give him her complete cooperation. With a harsh aggressiveness he bit at her nipples at the same time as he rammed his cock all the way inside her. He buried himself all the way to his balls and began vigorous strokes.

Rebecca gasped at his sudden attack. He wasn't being gentle or tender. His biting hurt her breasts, and his harsh assault frightened her. He was driving into her like a madman, using the entire length of his cock. On the downstroke he ground his pubic bone against hers and rotated his hips, stretching her pussy to its limit. She didn't understand why he was doing this to her. She pushed against his shoulders, trying to get his mouth away from her nipples.

Her voice quavered as she tried to talk to him. "Please, Gunthar, you're hurting me. Stop."

He heard her words but didn't acknowledge them. She was so hot and so tight. He now understood Edward's obsession with her. He released her nipple from his mouth. He wanted to watch her face; he needed to see the capitulation in her eyes, the acceptance of her submissive status, the verification of her acquiescence. More importantly, he wanted her to know that she was his for the moment, and that he was going to fuck her in every way possible. He was almost out of control.

She saw the lust in his eyes and knew he was going to have his way with her, no matter what. The complete horror of Jason's rape of her returned with startling abruptness. She had thought that horror was now behind her. Edward had shown her how incredible sex could be; now Gunthar was dredging up all her old fears.

Her nipples hurt where he had bitten into them. She tried to move her hips with him, slow down his frenzy as he drilled into her, bring back some kind of tenderness. Her fists clenched into hard knots as she pounded them against his chest. Tears streamed down her cheeks. She would rather be dead than endure this. Then, as suddenly as it had begun, the frantic urgency ceased. Gunthar closed his eyes and allowed his movements to slow into a sensual rhythm.

For the first time in quite a while Gunthar had almost completely lost control. Dark urges had risen inside him. He had caught himself just as he was about to slip over the edge. Rebecca wasn't his toy to do with as he wished; she was business and Edward's personal property. He hoped he hadn't done too much psychological damage. Edward would be furious if his loss of control had caused a setback. He would have to do whatever he could to smooth it over. He would deal with his urges later that night when he and Elsa were alone.

Gunthar's voice was thick and ragged as he spoke, all the time fucking Rebecca using a slow, smooth rhythm. "That's a sample of what could happen to you. Do you understand how important it is for you to be cooperative? With cooperation comes enjoyment." He gently sucked on the same nipple he had so recently bitten, licking around the peak before taking it into his mouth. "And now that you've experienced such joys often enough, you know that it only gets better and better." He was relieved to feel some of the tension drain away from her body.

He felt the churning in his balls. His intended lesson for this session was for her to suck his cock and swallow all of his sperm. That had been first on Edward's list of necessary accomplishments before his return. He needed to get back on schedule.

He pulled completely out of her and moved his body up hers until he straddled her shoulders. His erection bobbed in front of her mouth. "Take it, Rebecca. Take it into your mouth. I know you've never sucked on a prick before. I want the feel of your warm, wet mouth, the feel of your lips sliding up and down my shaft. Use your tongue. Lick it. Lick off all your pussy juices. Lick my cock head, roll your tongue all around it. Suck it, Rebecca. Suck it just like you did Elsa's clit, just like you did Edward's finger."

Rebecca was rapidly sinking into the throes of passion despite Gunthar's harsh treatment of her. She would gladly take anything into her mouth just to keep the delicious sensations building inside her. Her tongue fluttered out and dabbed at the drops of moisture on the tip of his prick. She tasted the salty liquid. She wanted more.

She was a little uncertain about how to proceed, how she was supposed to take his rod into her mouth. She swabbed his cock head with her tongue, licking all around the swollen cap and across the slit in its tip. The taste and texture was not at all what she had expected. Her body tingled each time her tongue touched the velvety skin. It was all so forbidden and sinful and so very exciting. A man's hard organ in her mouth—she never thought anything like that would ever be a reality.

"That's it, Rebecca." Gunthar's breath came in hard puffs as his own level of excitement heightened to a new plateau. "Run the tip of your tongue all the way along the underside of my prick, all the way to my balls."

Once she had given up conscious control of her emotions and sensual desires, she was only too eager to engage in whatever new activity was presented to her. A whole new world awaited her, a whole new reality and perspective of pleasure. How could she have let herself be shut away from all this for so long? She skimmed her tongue along the length of his organ, laving the hard ridge as he had instructed.

Her tongue touched his balls. What a totally different and tantalizing texture they had. She licked them, then took them into her mouth one at a time and held them there. Her arm reached around his hips and her fingers danced across his bottom. She wrapped her other hand around his stiff shaft and continued to tease his balls with her mouth. She scraped her fingers through the wiry growth on his belly, then again encircled his pole. It seemed to pulse in her hand.

A quick dose of reality darted through Gunthar's

consciousness. She was driving him to the edge. He needed to regain control. The purpose of this exercise wasn't fun and games: it was supposed to be a teaching session. She had adapted to the oral pleasures so quickly, however, that he wasn't sure exactly what he needed to be teaching her.

His breathing was ragged as he spoke. "That's so very good, so very nice. Take my prick into your mouth, Rebecca. Take my entire prick into your mouth. Suck on it, suck on it until I squirt all my cream down your throat. Take as much of me down your throat as you can."

She was almost beside herself. Her fervor drove her on. Her hips bucked wildly as the spasms passed through her pussy, even though nothing and no one was touching it. Her mouth was hungry for the taste of his cock and his sperm. She continued to hold on to his hard shaft, steadying his enormous cock head in front of her mouth. She slid her wet lips over the head and closed her mouth around it.

Somewhere in the back of her consciousness she heard him growl as he began to gently thrust his organ into her mouth. The texture and feel of his erection against her tongue and along the top of her mouth, the way her chin brushed his balls as he pushed into her and almost down her throat, was too much for her sensibilities to handle; she burst into a powerful orgasm. Gunthar reached behind his back and shoved two fingers up her pussy as she continued to convulse.

He was very near his own orgasm. He hadn't been prepared for her to actually climax just from having his cock in her mouth, with no direct stimulation of her pussy. He felt her convulsions subside, her body quiet down. His cock was still in her mouth. She had never let up on the sucking motion that seemed calculated to drain him dry. He felt his balls churning and tightening, then the irresistible rush of his semen.

His hot cream filled her mouth. His voice was husky as he gave her instructions. "Swallow it, Rebecca, all of it! Don't waste a single drop."

His instructions were unnecessary. She eagerly swallowed all he had to give. His sperm shot down her throat in four great spurts. And even then it appeared that she wanted more as she licked his cock clean. His cock was still hard as she milked him of every last drop.

This new delight sent waves of excitement through Rebecca: the taste of his cream, the way it spurted into her mouth, the hardness of his shaft, the texture of his balls. She knew she wanted more of this, much more. Any anxieties she was still harboring about Gunthar, and what he would make her do, and what he might do to her, had disappeared.

Gunthar gently subdued her enthusiastic lingual attack. He wanted to move along to something else and also wanted to get her inside out of the sun. "Come with me, Rebecca. Let's move to the bed." He stood next to her and extended his hand to help her up.

He situated himself on his back in the middle of the large bed, his cock undiminished. "Get on your knees, face me and straddle my legs."

She quickly complied with his instructions. Her entire being was in a heightened state of arousal, eager to experience whatever new delight he would introduce. She felt a tingling sensation in her pussy, and her breathing became ragged. She reached out and touched his prick, the hardness exciting her senses. She didn't know what was going to happen, but she was anxious to find out.

Her body glistened from a combination of the

suntan lotion and her perspiration. Droplets of moisture clung to her hard nipples. Her flaxen hair was in wild disarray with several loose tendrils matted against her damp face. Passion burned in her blue eyes.

Gunthar spent a very long minute absorbing the heated aura that surrounded her. She looked wild, untamed, free, and so very desirable. Edward's instincts had never been more on target than when he had chosen Rebecca Esterbrook to be his lover.

Gunthar clasped his hands around her hips and lifted her forward, positioning her ready cunt above his cock. He lowered her slowly onto his erection. His blood raced hot through his veins as he watched the expression of ecstasy cross her face. Her eyes closed, and her hands moved to her breasts to manipulate her nipples as she was impaled. She whimpered and moaned with delight as each inch of his cock passed between her delicate, pink pussy lips and disappeared into her love tunnel.

Tremors of excitement coursed through Rebecca's body. Gunthar's organ was so hard, so hot, and felt so good deep inside her. She was immediately aware of how deeply he penetrated her, how being on top of him gave her added stimulation for her throbbing clit. She felt powerful, forceful, in control of what was happening. Not waiting for his instructions, she took command of the situation. Exhibiting a new-found confidence, she rocked back and forth on his cock, rubbing her clit against his pubic bone.

Gunthar was pleased with what was happening. She had taken over, aggressively exerted herself, openly displayed her desires. He felt her pussy muscles squeezing his cock, her gyrations becoming more and more uninhibited. She was riding him like she had been doing it all her life. He slid his hands up her rib cage and cupped her breasts, allowing her to lean forward into his palms.

Rebecca was clearly a woman lost in the throes of wanton lust. Nothing mattered to her except the delicious sensations emanating from her hot cunt. Her body moved faster. She pushed against him harder. She gasped for air as orgasm after orgasm ripped through her body.

She no longer knew who she was, didn't know where she was. All she cared about were the intense explosions taking place deep inside her, one after the other. She didn't want them to ever stop. Her body jumped and jerked as she continued her wild gyrations. She tightened her pussy muscles, exulting in the way she could alter the tempo of his passion, and her own. She felt so powerful, so totally in control of the situation, yet at the same time, so out of control.

Gunthar couldn't withstand the onslaught of her incendiary passion much longer. He felt himself rushing to orgasm much sooner than he intended. He had wanted to maintain his arousal without going over the edge until she had totally exhausted herself and collapsed in a heap against his body. Then, and only then, would he allow himself his release. Unfortunately, that didn't seem to be the way things were going to happen.

Then, to his surprise and relief, she let out one last scream and sank into a whimpering heap on top of him. His body stiffened, shuddered, and the spasms raced through him as he shot a geyser of sperm into her already-drenched love box. Her body was completely limp, her labored breathing and pounding heart the only indications that she was even alive.

After bringing his own breathing under control, he

tried to bring her back to reality. He lifted her off his limp organ. Her entire pussy was sopping wet and very shiny—the suntan lotion, her perspiration, her pussy juices and his semen all combined to make a glistening sheen that covered both of their pubic areas. Their nectar trickled from her gaping cunt down her inner thighs. He traced her pussy lips, then touched his finger to her clit. Intense heat radiated from between her legs.

She jerked away from his hand, the ferocity of the sensation more than she could handle. Her entire pussy, especially her clit, was so sensitive even the slightest pressure caused her to cry out. She felt as though her entire body had been consumed by flames.

Gunthar was finally able to speak. "You did that very well. There's no way anyone would suspect it was your first time on top. It's different—a different emotional and psychological feeling as well as a physical one. Do you like being on top more than being on the bottom? Of everything you've experienced so far, Rebecca, which did you enjoy the most? What's given you the most pleasure?"

Rebecca continued to gasp for air. She felt totally drained and exhausted. Her pussy still tingled, her heart still pounded. She tried to speak. "I...don't know...can't think...very thirsty."

Gunthar left the bed and brought her a glass of water. He watched as she gulped it down without pausing. She handed him the empty glass then collapsed back on the bed. "That won't do, Rebecca. I've started the bath water. Come on, we'll bathe then have some lunch. After that, you can take a nap."

Without further comment, he led her into the bathroom and got into the large tub with her. Twenty minutes later they appeared on the patio where Elsa had set out the lunch. Conversation was light and casual, mostly between Elsa and Gunthar. Rebecca was too tired to eat. She was also too tired to notice the malevolent looks he directed her way, looks immediately noticed by Elsa. Rebecca very much wanted the nap Gunthar had mentioned.

Elsa escorted Rebecca back to her bedroom. During lunch the bed sheets had been changed and the bathroom cleaned. Rebecca removed the shorts and top she had put on following her bath and flopped across the bed. Before Elsa could say anything, Rebecca was asleep. Elsa locked the door to the suite, in case Rebecca woke up and tried to leave the room.

She rejoined Gunthar on the patio, carefully watching him. "Well, darling, it appears that you thoroughly exhausted our guest. Did everything go to your satisfaction?"

"Better than I could have hoped. I thought I was going to have to start from scratch with her, teach her a lesson in obedience before we could continue. Fortunately, Edward accomplished so much with her attitude and fears that it wasn't the case. And," he leaned across the table and gave Elsa a quick kiss, "it was our guest who almost exhausted me. She rode my prick until I was afraid I wouldn't be able to hold back long enough for her to exhaust herself. She almost fucked me into an early grave. It was the best pussy I've ever had…except for yours, of course."

Elsa leaned over and flicked her tongue in and out of his mouth. "Of course, darling. Besides, it's very important for people to enjoy their work."

They shared a moment of spontaneous laughter, then turned their attention to other matters. Elsa filled him in on the latest communication from

Edward. "His people have located Jason, and he has come up with an idea for a very interesting method of adjusting Jason's attitude. Before he proceeds though, we need to find out exactly what Rebecca's thoughts and plans are toward Randall Carpenter. If she has dismissed him as viable husband material, then Edward wants to hold off on the tape we have and go ahead with his plan."

Gunthar looked over the fax from Edward. A smile tugged at the corners of his mouth. He handed the paper to Elsa. "It looks like I'd better check out the inner sanctum and send someone into the village to find Topu."

His face suddenly reflected the harsh lust that had earlier threatened to take over his self-control. Elsa saw the sinister darkness come into his eyes. She reached out and touched his cheek. "I thought you seemed awfully close to the edge when you started with Rebecca. She excites you that much?"

His voice was thick and husky as he wrapped his hand around her upper arm. "The bitch excites me almost as much as you do." Without saying another word he roughly yanked Elsa through a connecting door into another room.

The inner sanctum was a windowless room that more closely resembled a castle dungeon than something found in a villa on a tropical island. In the middle of the room was a raised platform. Surrounding the platform were small tables on which were arrayed various implements. The walls were thickly padded and the ceiling mirrored. The entire room was totally soundproof.

Elsa's body trembled with a combination of fear and excitement. She knew what was going to happen, knew the delicious pleasure would outweigh the pain. When something propelled Gunthar into one of his dark moods he simply had to be satisfied.

He ripped Elsa's clothes from her. Then he shackled her body against the wall, her back to him with her arms high above her head and her legs wide apart. He quickly removed his own clothes. His cock was as hard as steel and a deep, red color, the bulbous head larger than normal. It bobbed before him as he moved quickly to a closet and removed a whip, a weapon he handled with incredible accuracy and skill.

NINE

A moment later a swish followed by a loud crack
sounded through the stilled air, and the tongue of the
leather lash nipped Elsa's left buttock, leaving a mere
speck of a mark. Gunthar cracked the whip again,
leaving an identical mark on her right cheek. She
flinched at the impact but didn't utter a sound. He
continued to alternate from her left cheek to her
right cheek, each mark landing a bit closer to the
long slit separating the hemispheres of her beautiful,
quivering bottom. Elsa knew it was only the beginning.

The lashes were coming faster and faster, continuing
with unbelievable accuracy. Each mark appeared
exactly where Gunthar intended. Soon Elsa's bottom

was stippled with what appeared to be a rash of insect bites.

Gunthar, breathing heavily, threw down the whip and picked up a leather strap. A moment later the back of her thighs felt the lash. Red welts began to appear on her smooth skin. Then the welts rose on her back when Gunthar shifted his attention.

Elsa could hold it in no longer. Her whimpers turned to groans, and finally to cries and screams of pain. Tears ran down her cheeks and she gasped for air. At the same time, however, a tremor of excitement churned deep inside her belly.

A thin layer of perspiration coated Elsa's body, and a sticky dampness matted her pussy fur. The tremor of excitement turned to spasms that raced through her cunt. Through her sobs she managed to say, "Gunthar…"

Hearing his name acted as a trigger. He threw the strap down, unshackled Elsa and watched as she sank to the floor. Not allowing her even a moment's rest, he picked her up and shoved her onto a thick, rubber mat.

He was clearly out of control. His hands squeezed her breasts, his fingernails leaving ugly scratches. His knees thrust her legs apart until they were spread wide. His breathing came in harsh gasps as he rammed his aching cock deep inside her cunt. He felt her searing heat as he slammed in and out of her opening, each forward thrust embedding his cock all the way to the balls.

His mouth found hers, and he bit at her lower lip until he tasted the warm saltiness of blood. He continued to slam his cock deep inside her cunt with a vicious intensity. He sucked a hardened nipple into his mouth and nipped at it, then bit into the firm flesh of her breast, leaving teeth marks. His fingers dug roughly into her rib cage.

162

Elsa cried out, her pain mixed with passion. Her fingernails left long scratches across his back and bottom. Her pussy exploded in a violent orgasm, the convulsions feeling as if they were ripping her insides apart. It was the precise moment when pleasure and pain became one.

Gunthar pulled out of her, picked her up and carried her to a sawhorse covered with thick padding. He leaned her across it, grabbed her bruised ass cheeks, spread them apart and jammed his cock deep inside her. His fingers dug into her cheeks as he slammed in and out of her asshole. Before his fevered eyes hung an image of Rebecca, naked, helpless, inviting.

For almost two hours he alternated strapping Elsa and violently ravishing her. He was totally possessed and unaware of what he was doing. He didn't sink into these dark pits of lust very often, but when he did there was nothing Elsa could do but endure the pain until he regained his senses.

Gunthar gave one final plunge into her anus, let out a scream and collapsed across her back as his hot cream gushed into her. He had difficulty catching his breath as he regained his composure slowly, becoming aware of his actions. He lifted his weight off Elsa and watched as she sank to the floor. His eyes finally focused on her battered body.

He visibly flinched as he surveyed the damage he had inflicted on her—the red welts on her back and legs, the whip marks on her buttocks, the teeth marks and scratches on her breasts, and the laceration on her lower lip. There had been several times when he had hurt her far worse, but it still upset him each time he saw the results of his descent into passion-induced madness.

He knelt beside her and cradled her trembling

body in his arms. "Elsa, honey. Are you all right?" He smoothed the errant tendrils of hair away from her face and tenderly kissed her mouth. He wiped the tears from her cheeks and kissed her eyelids.

Gunthar picked her up in his arms and carried her to their room. He ran bathwater and placed her in the tub. Carefully and lovingly he tended to her injuries, then laid her in bed so she could sleep. He left the bedroom. He had things to do and was behind schedule.

Rebecca had been napping the entire time and had no inkling of the dark abyss out of which Gunthar had just climbed. She woke when he gently shook her shoulder. "We have work to do, Rebecca." He was naked. He stretched out on the bed next to her and immediately began caressing her breasts and teasing her nipples. He gently toyed with one nipple as he sucked gently on the other. Her response to his stimulation was immediate; a warm wave surged through her body and her pussy muscles contracted each time he sucked on her tit.

The cold, frightened woman who arrived on the island with Edward no longer existed. Her feelings, emotions and sensuous inner being had been unleashed. She purred softly as Gunthar slipped his finger between her pussy lips. She reached her hand to his cock and wrapped her fingers around the hardening shaft.

"No, this is all wrong. You're in the wrong position, Rebecca. Turn around and stretch out on top of me. Put that sweet pussy where I can feast on it and wrap your lips around my prick." She moved to follow his instructions.

Gunthar felt her excitement as she licked his shaft, tickled his balls, and finally took his cock between her lips. She had become very adept at fellatio in a very short time. Her tongue swabbed the swollen head; she sucked quietly as she cradled his balls.

He slowly traced her small opening by trailing his finger between her outer and inner pussy lips. He finally spread the delicate folds apart. He inhaled the scent of her femininity and flicked his tongue at her clit. He smiled, snuggled back into the softness of the bed and prepared for a lengthy session of slowly feasting on her delicious cunt. He licked her mount until it was sopping wet, plastering the pale hairs against her flesh so that they seemed invisible. He moved down to her slit, slicing across the pink folds and teasing her by circling her entrance without penetrating her.

"Oh, please," Rebecca murmured. "Please, fuck me with your hot, wet tongue. Lick my clit. Let me feel your tongue inside me."

Gunthar smiled and continued his measured oral treatment of her. He began to approach her love button, but retreated before licking it, until Rebecca writhed and begged him to take it in his mouth. He circled it, lapped all around it, then finally flicked at it.

Rebecca gasped and closed her eyes as the first waves of intense pleasure filled her. She swallowed his cock again, licking the head and allowing it to slip in almost as far as her throat. She pumped it with her mouth, pausing only to take a deep breath as he now earnestly tended to her clitty. When he took it fully into his mouth and began to suck on it, she lost track of everything.

Rebecca's body shook from the prolonged intensity of Gunthar's lingual assault. The sensations had been going on for what seemed like hours. She had no idea how many orgasms had enveloped her, they seemed to follow one after the other.

She loved having his cock in her mouth, loved every sensation: the rippled texture of his balls, the softness of the rounded helmet, the hardness of his shaft, the salty taste of the liquid that occasionally leaked from the tip.

Gunthar had managed to hold back his orgasm. He wasn't finished with her, didn't want to be finished with her. Her taste was the nectar of life; he simply could not get enough of it. Her juices flowed freely, as if a faucet had been turned on and left to run.

He knew he needed to expand his stimulation of her body, not just devour her pussy. His fingers moved across her ass, tickled and massaged her cheeks, then trailed up and down her separation. He had to stop thinking only of his own enjoyment and get on with the business at hand.

He reached for the bottle of massage oil next to the bed and applied it generously to her entire bottom. Again he trailed his finger up and down the separation of her ass cheeks pausing each time his finger passed over her anus. He continued to suck on her engorged clit and thrust his tongue deep inside her pussy.

He slowly slipped one finger into her anus. He felt her jump as he penetrated the hard ring of muscle, but she didn't try to pull away. He worked the finger in and out of her rosebud opening until he sensed a difference in her movements. She was no longer solely grinding her pussy against his mouth. Her response now included wiggling her bottom against his hand.

Gunthar added a second finger, causing her to jump and gasp at the intrusion. He wanted to stretch the opening to eventually accommodate something much larger. He worked quickly. He knew he couldn't last too much longer. With each new stimulation he introduced to her body, her mouth and hands automatically responded with increased fervor on his tight balls and hard organ.

He thrust the two fingers in and out of her anus with greater speed and urgency as he withdrew his mouth from her steaming cunt. He heard her whimper of dismay at the loss of the attention to her pussy. She pushed and wiggled her ass more vigorously against his hand to regain some of the lost sensations.

Then it happened. Rebecca felt a whole new set of intense sensations building around her anus and inside her belly. An entirely different type of orgasm surged through her body. As soon as the waves commenced she felt Gunthar's body stiffen. Her mouth was flooded with his hot sperm; she could feel the spasms with each hard spurt. She greedily gulped every drop.

Her ass tingled with excitement, her puckered asshole clutched his two fingers. Neither Gunthar nor Rebecca moved for a long minute. Gradually their breathing came under control. He slowly withdrew his fingers and rolled her off his body.

His face was slick with her pussy juices, and his cock was still very hard in spite of his massive orgasm. He knew Edward was going to be very pleased when he returned. Rebecca had responded openly and enthusiastically to every new thing and every new concept. He would have anal intercourse with her after dinner. It would be a fairly brief session. He knew how exhausted she must be; there hadn't been time for her to build up any stamina for prolonged fucking sessions.

Elsa had been correct again; Rebecca would be the very best of their converts. He allowed his mind to momentarily wander to the twin virgins that would be given to Elsa and him as their bonus. His cock jumped and twitched as a mental picture began to form.

"We have time for something else before preparing for dinner." Gunthar had allowed Rebecca a few minutes rest. Now he turned her over onto her stomach. His cock was still hard and his face still shone with her pussy juices. "Pull your knees up under you. I want that yummy pussy and beautiful ass up in the air so I can enjoy them."

A shiver of anxiety passed through her, but she immediately obeyed his orders. She was still a little nervous about having her bottom so exposed and vulnerable even though he had just made her feel wonderful. The memory of Jason viciously brutalizing her, causing her so much pain, terror and humiliation, still lingered.

Gunthar moved his hand between her legs, cupping her entire pussy. The intense heat still radiated from her dripping slit. He tucked his body up close behind hers and teased her pussy lips with the tip of his cock. Her response to this stimulation was immediate; she pushed back against him and moaned softly.

He edged into her love box with excruciating slowness until his prick was finally buried up to his balls. Before he could begin shuttling in and out of her tunnel she exploded into orgasm. She was so hot and ready that any titillation at all sent her over the edge. He hadn't even reached around her hips to touch her clit. Just the new experience of having her cunt entered from behind did it.

Her vaginal muscles grabbed at his organ as she convulsed into yet another orgasm. The magnitude of what her body was going through was too overwhelming for her to consciously deal with—her mind became a complete blank. Her last clear thought was about the possibility of actually overdosing on sex as if it were a lethal drug.

Gunthar continued to pump into her from behind. Each stroke brought his pelvis up tight against her bottom so that his thick pubic hair tickled her ass. His fingers kneaded her firm buttocks. He pumped in and out of her cunt with increased vigor as he slipped two fingers up her anus and wiggled them back and forth.

Rebecca's ass twitched completely out of control. Her pussy felt as though it was on fire while her juices flowed in an effort to put out the flames. Between sobs she managed to gasp: "Please...no more...not right now...must rest...too much..."

Gunthar slammed into her hard and fast to bring on his own orgasm before Rebecca actually passed out from the intensity of the sensations coursing through her body. He shuddered and gave one last plunge into her, unleashing everything that had been churning in his balls.

Rebecca collapsed on the bed, her body limp. She couldn't move; she was barely able to breathe.

Gunthar pulled his cock from her soaked pussy and climbed off the bed. Rebecca didn't acknowledge the fact that he no longer filled her love nest.

Rebecca's body had been through an overwhelming physical upheaval. For three days she had been subjected to almost nonstop intense stimulation of a type that she had never before experienced. She felt totally drained of energy. Her pussy was extremely tender, overly sensitive to any touch. Only her continual state of extreme arousal allowed her to disregard the soreness of her flesh. She fell into an exhausted sleep, not even caring about cleaning up and refreshing herself.

Gunthar hurried down the hall toward his bedroom. Elsa was awake but still in bed. He sat down next to her, kissing her tenderly on the mouth. With a light, loving touch he placed a fingertip on her lacerated lip. "Does it hurt very much?"

She looked lovingly into his caring eyes. "It's not too bad. It should be fine in a day or two."

"You know how sorry I am. It was Rebecca—I was so turned on by her that I couldn't help myself." He placed another tender kiss on her mouth. "I'll make it up to you. You know I will."

"I know." She settled into his warm embrace as they snuggled in silence.

Dinner was delayed by two hours. Elsa needed more rest, and both Elsa and Gunthar agreed that Rebecca needed to sleep. They turned their attention to business and discussed a regimen of exercise for increasing Rebecca's stamina so that she would be able to handle long sessions of uninterrupted sexual activity. They were both thoroughly aware of Edward's voracious appetite. Besides, Rebecca didn't spend enough time outdoors enjoying the sun. She needed to swim, play tennis, take walks on the beach. She was too pale, appeared too fragile—she seemed out of place on the island.

Rebecca awoke on her own. She remained quiet for a few minutes, trying to make sense of everything that had happened to her, trying to sort out what was real. She realized with some small surprise that she missed Edward's lovemaking. Gunthar had introduced her to exciting new things and driven her to new heights of arousal, but Edward had made love to her.

She now recognized and understood the difference. Even though Gunthar was not indifferent to her pleasure, he had never kissed her. With him it had been sex for the sake of sex. Edward said he wanted her to be his lover, not his sex slave. She looked forward to the time when he would return to the island.

Rebecca finally got out of bed, bathed and dressed. She felt a little more rested and was definitely hungry. She had only picked at her lunch. She was surprised to find the door open. She left the suite and started for the dining patio. It was the first time she had been outside her suite unescorted.

She wandered outside. The table was set for dinner but Elsa and Gunthar weren't there. She sat down and waited. She didn't know what else to do.

"Well, you're awake and up. We didn't want to disturb you, you needed the rest." Elsa's voice was upbeat, friendly, as she and Gunthar walked out onto the patio.

Rebecca turned around at the sound of her voice. Elsa was dressed in long pants and a blouse that completely covered her upper body. Her face was a little drawn and her lower lip was swollen and appeared to be cut. Gunthar had his arm around her and seemed to be supporting her, helping her to the table. An inner voice told her that something was wrong and that she had better not ask about it.

"Dinner will be ready in a few minutes." Gunthar addressed his comments to Rebecca. "Let's have a glass of wine." He held a chair for Elsa so she could sit down. Rebecca noted the fact that neither of them made any untoward advances or comments to her, didn't try to touch her in a sexual way. It was as if she were a houseguest or business associate.

Things were becoming much clearer. Elsa and Gunthar were Edward's employees. This was their job. This was a period of rest, not work. She smiled inwardly as she wondered what their job functions would be called on a resume—probably something like "personal services."

Dinner progressed in a pleasant and casual manner. The three of them engaged in friendly and open conversation about a number of topics—art, travel, theater, literature. Rebecca was surprised at how knowledgeable both of them were in a variety of areas. Edward's words came back to her, his comments about the high regard he had for intelligence and education. Those requirements obviously extended to his employees as well.

As soon as they finished dinner Gunthar whisked Rebecca back to her bedroom. She knew that something else would be happening that night, but she couldn't imagine what it would be. She stood next to the bed waiting for Gunthar to indicate what he wanted of her. It was time for work again. Her body quivered in anticipation.

He removed her top and pulled her shorts down to her ankles where upon she immediately stepped out of them. His gaze took in every inch of her body before he made any move to touch her. Finally he cupped her breasts and teased her stiffening nipples. Without saying a word he bent his head and sucked first on one peak, then on the other. He felt the energy growing in her body as he aroused her desires.

Rebecca's entire body tingled with delight as his sensual mouth teased, nibbled and sucked on her tender breasts. She felt the dampness between her legs, felt it spread across her mound. She wanted more.

He cupped her breasts as he circled her, finally stopping behind her, his erection pressing against the separation of her bottom. "You have the most perfect tits; the size, the shape, the taste, the texture—they're absolutely perfect." He ground his hard cock against her ass while guiding her toward the bed. He laid her across the bed, face down, and reached for the massage oil.

Rebecca sighed softly as his nimble fingers massaged the oil across her shoulders, down her back and all over her bottom. His words again danced in her ears: "You also have the most beautiful ass." His fingers separated her cheeks and trailed along the crack. He bent forward and ran his tongue along the same path, pressing it against her rosebud opening. She barely quivered. He was very pleased. This next step would be accomplished without any problems.

He thoroughly oiled her anus and started to apply a generous amount to his own hard cock, then changed his mind. He would have her do it instead. He left her where she was and repositioned himself on his haunches in front of her. "Hold out your hands. I'm going to pour some oil into them. I want you to rub it into my prick until it glistens."

She complied with his wishes, stroking his shaft gently. She allowed some of the oil to dribble onto his balls. She rolled his hard shaft between her palms and teased the head. She impulsively flicked out her tongue and touched it to the very tip of his organ. He pulled away from her, his voice husky. "That's not the lesson for tonight."

He moved back behind her, separated her legs and knelt between them. With firm, strong hands he lifted her hips until her rear end bobbed enticingly in the air. She instinctively pulled her knees up under her and continued to lean forward on her elbows. She knew what he was going to do, but it no longer frightened her.

Gunthar inserted two fingers into her asshole and moved them around. She responded by shoving back against his hand. He thrust his fingers in and out in a slow rhythm for a few moments, then withdrew them completely.

"There may be a bit of discomfort for a moment, though I'll try not to hurt you." He placed the slippery head of his cock against her well-lubricated rosebud and gently pushed past her opening. She jumped and let out a little cry but didn't try to pull away from him. He paused to let her assimilate the feeling.

He slowly and carefully inserted the entire length of his shaft into her anal canal. When he was buried up to his balls he again paused to allow her a moment to become accustomed to accommodating his organ. Holding her hips, he began a smooth stroking rhythm. He moved in and out of her, thrilling to the tightness that encased his organ.

Rebecca was at first startled by how large he felt as his cock head entered her followed by his entire length. After the pleasure she had realized just that afternoon when he had penetrated her with his fingers, she hadn't been sure what to expect when he inserted his cock into her. It had slid in smoothly and fairly comfortably, not at all like Jason's smaller organ that he'd rammed up her without using any lubrication at all.

Gunthar increased the length of his strokes and the speed of his rhythm. His balls slapped her drenched pussy lips. Her ass was delightful, almost as good as Elsa's. He continued pumping her with even thrusts as her excitement grew. Her ass wiggled against his pelvis, pushing back against each of his forward plunges.

He started to reach his arms around her and stimulate her clit, to help her associate the feel of his cock inside her ass with the pleasures of her pussy, but she was already responding so enthusiastically he decided he didn't need to provide the additional assistance. He closed his eyes, allowed a smile of utter contentment to curl his lips, and continued to pump her with a slightly more urgent rhythm.

Before long Rebecca was thrashing erratically on the bed, whimpering and aggressively shoving her bottom hard against his cock to tempt him into a faster rhythm. She wanted more, wanted it harder and faster. She got her wish. Gunthar pumped short jabs in and out of her as he felt the familiar tightening in his balls.

A final gasp escaped her throat as the convulsions spread quickly through her body. She felt Gunthar's body stiffen and shudder. She could feel his organ twitch with each spurt of his semen as he remained buried deep inside her ass. She collapsed on the bed with his body lying on top of hers.

After a few minutes he pulled his limp organ from her anus, moved down her body, separated her ass cheeks with his fingers and gently dabbed his tongue to her rosebud—tasting his cream as it oozed out. He inserted his finger into the wet opening and held it there as he spoke to her. "Your lessons are done for today. If you were being graded, I'd gladly rate you as being superior in all categories. Edward is going to be very pleased when he returns. Good night, Rebecca."

With that, Gunthar left her alone in the suite and returned to Elsa. He took a quick shower and joined Elsa in bed. He wrapped his arms around her and captured her mouth with a loving, comfortable kiss. He twined his fingers in her pussy fur as he darted his tongue into her mouth. Her tongue fluttered against his. They slowly and sensually made love, each giving totally to the pleasure of the other.

Rebecca awoke early the next morning feeling fully rested and looking forward to what the day would bring. Gunthar's words of praise still echoed in her ears. Not only had she acquired the skills of love-making, she had been told by an expert that she had become very proficient in the execution of those skills. She felt very pleased with herself. She even gave a brief thought to making Jason eat his words about her being totally inadequate to fulfill the needs of a man.

The soft warmth of the morning sun seemed so very inviting. She settled back on the chaise longue on her private patio and applied suntan lotion to her front. She closed her eyes as a gentle breeze tickled her skin. In the distance she could hear waves breaking along the beach. She felt totally relaxed and at peace with the world.

Not more than five minutes later, Elsa entered the bedroom to see if Rebecca was awake. She spotted her sunning herself, completely nude, on the patio. She grinned as she thought about how far Rebecca had come in only a few days. She went to Rebecca's closet, picked out a bright red, string bikini and took it to her.

"Here, put this on and we'll go for a walk along the beach. You haven't been outside the villa since we arrived. It's really a very lovely island with a gorgeous white sand beach just on the other side of the wall. I'll put some lotion on your back." She handed the bikini to Rebecca as she studied her. "You picked up the start of a tan yesterday; the little bit of color looks good on you. You can work on it some more today."

Rebecca slipped into the tiny bathing suit and looked at herself in the mirror. She suppressed a grin. "As recently as a week ago there was no way I would have worn something this skimpy and revealing, even in private. Now look at me, I'm even sunning myself nude."

Elsa silently noted another change in Rebecca— her willingness to talk about herself and even make light of the situation. She concluded that this would probably be a very opportune time to see if she would open up about her intentions regarding Randall Carpenter, and to get a feel for how receptive she would be to getting revenge against Jason.

The two women had morning coffee and juice on the dining patio and were joined by Gunthar. He let out a loud whistle of appreciation and grinned lasciviously at Rebecca. "That's some bathing suit you're almost wearing. It looks great on you. If I didn't already know what it was hiding, I'd sure be hot to find out."

At first Rebecca was shocked by his words, but then she relaxed and joined in with the laughter. It was useless to be indignant about his insinuation, especially since her body no longer held any secrets or surprises. They finished their coffee, then left Gunthar on the patio and headed out the gate toward the beach. Rebecca made no mention of the fact that Elsa was still dressed in long pants and a blouse. Whatever had happened to her lip probably had some connection to the way she was dressed.

The warm sun and the balmy, tropical breeze filled Rebecca with a sense of contentment. The fine sand felt good squishing between her bare toes, while the gentle waves lapped at her toes and occasionally splashed her ankles. Every now and then she would stop and pick up a sea shell. She felt almost like a kid again, unencumbered and free.

Elsa cautiously broached the subject of Jason. "Your ex-husband...have you ever wished there was some way to get even with him for what he did to you, some way to make him suffer as much as he's made you suffer?"

Rebecca remained silent for a long moment, a pensive look covering her face and the emotional pain showing in her eyes. Finally she spoke, carefully measuring her words. "For a long time it was what I wanted more than anything. I even imagined a time when my family would be back on its feet financially and I could pay someone to do something to him. I've always felt ashamed afterward for thinking such a terrible thing, but it doesn't stop the thought from coming back time and time again."

"You still think about it?"

"Not as much. I guess time eventually takes care of lots of things. Besides, my family never recovered from the financial losses, so my energies have been directed more toward that end."

"What do you mean?"

"There's a man in Boston that I was hoping to marry. His family wealth and position could put my family back on its feet again. So far, Randall hasn't shown any interest in getting married." Rebecca looked around as if making sure no one was within earshot, then continued: "The rumor is that he's gay, but I don't really know that for a fact. Besides, at the time I didn't think it would matter since sex was of no interest to me."

"What about now? Do you still want to marry him?"

Rebecca stopped walking and looked out across the water, shading her eyes with her hand. Her voice was small and uncertain. "I don't know. I don't know anything any more. What used to be real no longer is, and what was unreal is now a reality." She turned toward Elsa. "Besides, unless

Edward lets me go home what I want doesn't really matter."

"What if he were to take you home next week? Would you still want to marry Randall just to restore your family's fortune and position? What kind of a life do you think you'd have being married to him?"

They started walking again as Rebecca thought over the question. After several minutes of silence she finally answered. "No, I could not marry him now—not after what I've learned and experienced here. I know now that what I once thought I could live with would never work."

Elsa had the information she wanted. She casually turned the conversation to lighter matters as they started back to the villa. When they arrived brunch was waiting. Gunthar again joined them, and they enjoyed a leisurely meal. After lunch Rebecca excused herself, saying she felt hot and sticky and wanted to take a shower to wash off the suntan lotion and sand.

TEN

As soon as she was sure Rebecca was out of earshot, Elsa told Gunthar about the conversation they'd had while walking along the beach. "It looks like we can put the Randall Carpenter problem to rest. What do you think Edward's going to do about Jason?"

Gunthar was thoughtful. "I don't know. It could go either way. I think it will depend on how much of a hold it will give him on Rebecca. My guess is that he'll want to use her for special things in addition to just being his personal lover. After all, a beautiful blonde with a perfect body who is able to fulfill any fantasy is something some men lust after all their lives." He took Elsa's hand and they went down the hall to the security room.

Gunthar took a tape out of the safe, popped it into the VCR and pushed the play button. "Speaking of fantasies, I wonder how she would have reacted to this tape of Randall. He has a circle of gay sex contacts at home, but I guess if you're socially prominent there are certain chances you can't take." He turned toward Elsa as the picture came up on the monitor. "Have you ever heard Edward say how much Randall pays him to arrange these monthly sessions?"

"I have no idea, but it must be a bundle."

They both watched the monitor. A very tall woman dressed only in a black leather garter belt, black fishnet stockings, spike heels and carrying a riding crop, held a commanding position on a raised platform in the center of a bare, windowless room. Her long, black hair stood out in wild disarray. Even though her breasts were very large, they stood out and were capped with prominent nipples. Her pussy mound was shaved clean except for a line of dark fur one inch wide that extended upward from her clit.

Gunthar chuckled. "When Monica gets into that costume and puts on that wig it really transforms her. Sometimes she even frightens me. It amazes me that she can keep three and sometimes four different kinds of scenes going at one time. It has to drain her both emotionally and physically."

They continued to watch. A burly man wearing only a black leather jockstrap led Randall Carpenter into the room by a leash attached to a collar around his neck. Carpenter's wrists were bound in front of him with a black strap. He wore only a lavender lace bra and a pair of lavender lace panties. His erection strained against the front of the panties.

182

The burly man shoved Randall across a padded post set in the floor. He fastened Randall's wrists to a hook set in the floor, then spread his legs and fastened his ankles to the post legs. Randall squirmed and pulled against his restraints.

Monica stepped off the raised platform and slowly made her way to Randall. The burly man reached inside his jockstrap, pulled out a huge, limp cock and held it to Randall's lips. Randall shook his head from side to side and pursed his lips tightly together.

Monica's riding crop bit into Randall's shoulders and back, leaving ugly, red welts. Her voice was hard and cold. "Open your mouth, you disgusting little prick. Suck on that big cock until it's nice and hard." She ripped the panties from his body and viciously slashed the riding crop across his quivering ass until she drew blood, smiling cruelly as he screamed in pain.

Elsa smirked at the antics on the screen. She turned to Gunthar. "He always wants the same rape fantasy scene. He's tied up and forced to suck on Topu's cock. Then Topu fucks his ass until Randall screams for mercy. Then Randall shoots his load all over himself. The only thing that changes is the color of the panties and bra he wears and whether or not he wants Monica to only whip him or also sodomize him with that riding crop before Topu fucks him."

Gunthar stopped the tape, took it out of the VCR and replaced it in the safe. He grabbed Elsa's hand. "Do you feel up to a little three-way action with Rebecca before dinner, or would you rather wait until later?"

"I think it would be better if we waited until after dark. If we leave the lights off she'll be less likely to notice the marks on my body. She would never understand them, at least not yet. She's already suspicious. I can tell by the way she looks at me."

Rebecca finished drying off, wrapped the towel around herself and casually wandered into the sitting room. She poured herself a glass a white wine and carried it out onto the patio. She felt so comfortable, so at ease. She couldn't think of a time in her entire life when she felt more contented and free than she did at that moment. "Free" was an unusual word to associate with her circumstances, she reflected, but it fit the way she felt.

She allowed her mind to wander back to her conversation with Elsa. How odd it was that Elsa should bring up Jason. She hadn't consciously thought of revenge for a couple of years. Now that the thought had been reintroduced into her mind, however, she found it very appealing. How she would like to see him suffer the way he had made her suffer. She wanted to see him brutalized and humiliated.

Her thoughts were interrupted by Gunthar's voice. "That's a very intense expression you have on your face. Is something wrong?"

She hesitated for a moment. "No...nothing's wrong. I was just thinking."

"Whatever you were thinking couldn't have been too pleasant. Why don't we see if we can do something to put a smile on your face?" Gunthar slowly pulled on the towel that was tucked around her body. With very little effort he removed it and let it drop to the patio floor. He stepped aside and motioned for Rebecca to come back into the bedroom. She did so without hesitation. Her excitement built as Gunthar removed his clothes.

Rebecca didn't know where to begin—what to hold on to, put in her mouth, insert between her pussy lips or up her anus. Gunthar took the initiative, however, and decided to try a bit of everything. He began by having her kneel in front of him and take his cock in her mouth. She did so without hesitation, though she didn't take him down her throat, only as far into her mouth as she could. She licked him eagerly, laving the entire head of his cock and wrapping her lips tightly around the shaft as she pumped him. With one hand she cradled his balls; her other arm circled his waist and her hand rubbed his buttocks, settling into the cleft of his cheeks and finding his asshole.

Not wanting to become too excited at this stage of their activities, Gunthar pulled back from her and indicated that she should lie on the floor. When she did so, he moved between her legs. He brought his arms up below her knees and lifted them, his cock dangling before her pouting slit. The head of it found her opening without additional guidance, and he pushed into her, lodging half his length inside her. He reared back and thrust again, this time driving all of his cock into her until his balls slapped her upturned buttocks. He leaned into her so that he could reach her tits while he pumped her. He rolled her nipples between his fingers as his pelvis worked back and forth. He grinned as Rebecca began to moan softly and pushed up against him.

"You like that, don't you?" he said as he continued to crush her breasts while he fucked her. "There's nothing you won't do now—suck cock, take it in the pussy or up the ass, do yourself in front of others." He began to shuttle in and out harder and faster. "It's what Edward wanted...and now it's what you want, isn't it?" He banged against her bottom as he drove into her.

"Yes! Yes!" groaned Rebecca as she put her hands

over his and massaged her aching breasts. But before she could reach orgasm, Gunthar pulled out of her and turned her over on her knees.

"You know what's coming now, don't you?" Without another word, he steered his glistening prick to her anus and shoved it into her puckered opening.

Rebecca straightened up at the intrusion and her eyes started from her head as Gunthar began to ram his cock in and out of her asshole. Then she relaxed and, as a warm feeling settled over her, started to push back against him. He seemed pleased by this, and reached around and fondled her clit until she shook as her orgasm overcame her.

Gunthar grunted and pushed into her harder and harder. Her anal muscles grasped his cock so tightly that he knew he wouldn't last more than another minute. Eager to reach his climax, he slammed against her bottomcheeks until his cock seemed ready to explode. A moment later, his sperm geysered into Rebecca's warm tunnel. He was very pleased with her response and eager participation. He knew Edward would be very pleased. He left her to shower and dress.

The evening air carried the perfume of tropical flowers. Rebecca, Elsa and Gunthar lingered over drinks on the dining patio. It was very strange…these people who held her captive now seemed closer to her than almost anyone else. The only thing needed to make the evening perfect was Edward's presence. Rebecca wondered when he would return.

Following dinner the three of them returned to Rebecca's suite. Rebecca wondered why Gunthar insisted on leaving the lights off, but she didn't say anything. They undressed and stretched out on the bed together.

Elsa's touch was soft as she brushed her lips

against Rebecca's mouth. When Rebecca put her arms around Elsa, she felt the raised welts on her back. A little shiver ran through her. She wasn't sure what to make of it. She had heard about people who enjoyed pain, even found it sexually stimulating. She wondered if that was part of Elsa and Gunthar's relationship.

Elsa pulled Rebecca's face to her breast, a soft moan escaping her lips as Rebecca took the nipple into her mouth.

Everything was so exciting to Rebecca—the feel of Elsa's puckered nipple in her mouth, Elsa's lips brushing against the nape of her neck, Gunthar waiting to bury his cock deep inside her love tunnel. Any further thoughts about the welts on Elsa's back were erased from her mind.

Elsa and Gunthar maneuvered Rebecca into a position that she didn't think was possible. He lay on his back with Rebecca lying atop him. In a moment he had his cock firmly embedded in her anal canal, his arms enveloping her while his hands massaged her breasts and teased her nipples. Elsa lay on her stomach on top of Rebecca, her pussy at Rebecca's mouth and Rebecca's pussy at her mouth. The three of them were stacked up like a club sandwich.

Elsa's arms reached around Rebecca's thighs and Gunthar's hips until she was able to fondle his balls and insert a finger into his anus. Gunthar and Elsa guided Rebecca into a rhythm that allowed the two women to suck and lick each other's cunts while Gunthar plunged his cock in and out of Rebecca's asshole. Rebecca exploded, soaring through orgasm after orgasm, not knowing where one ended and the next one began.

Over the next three hours Elsa and Gunthar both marvelled at how totally uninhibited and free

Rebecca had become. She accepted each suggestion they made and everything they wanted her to try. There was nothing left for them to teach her.

Edward worked late in his office. His last task before leaving was setting in motion his plan for Jason. He read the confidential report he'd received one last time, then opened his desk drawer and took out his private phone. He dialed a local number and spoke quickly. "We will depart at two o'clock in the morning." That was all that needed to be said. He replaced the phone and left his office.

A black limo moved slowly down the darkened street in the unsavory neighborhood, the driver and two passengers keeping a sharp eye on the lone figure leaving a bar and making his way toward the parking lot. The limo pulled up to the curb as the man unlocked his car door.

With smooth proficiency the two passengers jumped from the limo, quickly subdued the man, blindfolded him and put a gag across his mouth. One of the passengers shoved the man into the back seat; the other took the man's keys and drove off in his car. The operation was efficiently concluded before anyone was even aware that something was happening.

The blindfolded, gagged man struggled against his much larger assailant, who had him pinned against the limo's floorboards. The larger man's voice was hard and impatient. "It's no use struggling, Jason. There is nothing and no one that can prevent what's going to happen to you."

The limo moved quickly through the night, arriving at the private airstrip. A jet was waiting on the tarmac. The large man pulled Jason out of the limo and maneuvered him toward the plane. Jason put up some initial resistance, but it was very obvious that he was scared. He was shoved into a chair, his hands tied behind his back and his ankles bound, then strapped in for takeoff.

They had been in the air for half an hour when Edward emerged from the plane's executive bedroom. He carried a file folder as he approached Jason, taking note of the man's disheveled appearance: shaggy unwashed hair, sloppy shirt and jeans, a patchy stubble of beard on his chin. He matched the look of the seedy bar from which they had abducted him.

His fall from the heights had been dizzying—from the outwardly charming, young man that any mother would have been pleased to have escort her daughter, to a twenty-nine-year-old has-been who made his living as a petty thief. Edward removed the blindfold and gag and looked him over with disdain. Finally he seated himself so that they faced each other.

Jason's gaze darted nervously around the plane before coming to rest on Edward. He recognized Edward's face but couldn't place it, couldn't attach it to a name. After a few minutes of nervous silence, Jason spoke. He tried to make his voice as tough and defiant as possible, but he failed miserably. "Who...who the fuck are you, and why the hell am I here?" He attempted to glare at Edward, but in that, too, he failed.

Edward's voice was calm but held a menacing edge. "I find people like you beneath contempt. You're the scum that lives in the gutter, the fungus that feeds on decaying matter." His words had the desired effect. He watched as Jason recoiled, almost as if he had been physically struck.

Edward opened the file folder and read aloud the report on Jason's sterling accomplishments from the age of eighteen to the present. When he finished he put the folder aside. "Married for three months—that's not a very long time. I think you should tell me about it." Edward leaned back in his chair and waited for Jason to speak.

For the next hour Edward grilled Jason on a variety of topics. Jason tried to maintain a tough facade, but he eventually caved in and told Edward everything he wanted to know. He was obviously very frightened and knew he was way out of his league—at the total mercy of this mysterious and unsettling man who spoke softly but whose eyes and manner projected immense power.

Edward rose from his seat, his tall frame towering over the cringing Jason. "I suggest you get some sleep. We'll be landing in a couple of hours, and you'll need all your strength and energy." He allowed a smirk to turn the corners of his mouth.

A cold shiver raced up Jason's spine as he watched Edward disappear through the door at the back of the plane. He had finally placed Edward's face. He had seen his picture in the newspaper plenty of times. This was a very rich and powerful man. Jason didn't like the hot anger that had flickered through Edward's eyes while he was telling him about his abbreviated marriage to that society bitch who turned out to be such a bum lay. Even more unsettling had been the dark malevolence that darted through Edward's eyes before he returned to the back of the plane.

The morning sky turned from orange to gold to a brilliant blue. Rebecca put on the string bikini and went to the pool. She felt comfortable now wandering through the villa on her own. She no longer felt that it was something she wasn't supposed to do. She did notice a couple of doors that had keypad security locks on them, but other than that, everything seemed to be available to her.

She stood on the first step of the stairs that led into the shallow end of the pool. The water felt warm. She continued to walk down the stairs until she arrived at the bottom, the water reaching to her hips. She ducked completely under the surface and shoved off. Her strokes were sure and confident.

Rebecca felt wonderful. It had been a long time since she had allowed herself the luxury of something as simple as getting her hair wet in a swimming pool. The water rushing over her skin invigorated her senses. The lethargy she had experienced over the past few years had completely disappeared. She was alive and vital once again. She swam laps for half an hour before stopping and climbing out of the pool. The balmy breeze hitting her wet skin caused a tingling sensation. She grabbed a towel and quickly patted the water off her body.

Elsa and Gunthar were seated on the patio having their morning coffee. Rebecca's new tan complemented the shine of her damp, blond tresses. The wet bikini clung to her body. Her hips swayed as she moved to join them at the table.

"Am I in time for breakfast?" Edward's smooth voice sent shivers through Rebecca as it floated from somewhere behind her. She spun around in her chair and saw him framed in the doorway. He wore white shorts and a white shirt that accentuated the tan on his athletic body. Her only thought at that moment was how gorgeous he looked, how absolutely delicious.

Edward seated himself next to Rebecca. Before anything else, he gave instructions to Gunthar and Elsa. "See to our guest...and don't let him touch anything until you've cleaned him up—he must live in a pigsty or a garbage dump. He's a filthy mess. Jack is going to have to air out the jet and clean the seat our guest was sitting in before he can start back."

As soon as Elsa and Gunthar left the table Edward turned his attention to Rebecca. He ran his fingertips along her cheek and down the side of her neck. His voice was slightly husky. "I see you've gotten the start of a nice tan. It looks good on you." He saw the desire in her blue eyes and immediately felt the warmth of her body. He knew, absolutely knew, that the Ice Maiden was gone. He leaned forward and pressed his mouth to hers.

Rebecca's response was immediate. Her tongue darted and twined with his, her arms circled his neck, her fingers slipped through his thick hair. Her kiss was hot and passionate, her body supple and accommodating. Yes—this was exactly what he wanted, exactly what he hoped he would find upon his return to the island. Gunthar said things had gone very well, had told him he would be pleased. Gunthar had been correct.

Rebecca melted in his arms. Her pulse raced as his mouth captured hers. Her entire body tingled with sweet anticipation. She wanted him; she craved his lovemaking more than food, more than the air she breathed, more than life. She murmured in his ear, "I've missed you, Edward. Make love to me, now—please, Edward. Right now."

Without further discussion, they went immediately to Rebecca's suite. She tugged urgently at his clothes, pulling his shirt off over his head and lowering his shorts so he could step out of them. She immediately dropped to her knees and caressed his erection. Everything she had learned was put into practice.

She cradled his balls while she teased his cock with

her tongue. She swabbed the head then ran the tip of her tongue along the complete length of the underside of his shaft. She sampled the tantalizing texture of his balls and drew them into her mouth, holding them there for a moment before releasing them. She licked his entire rod, her tongue leaving shiny trails of saliva. Then she took him into her mouth and began a gentle sucking.

A growl escaped from deep inside Edward. Her mouth was doing amazing things. His breathing quickened as his whole body tensed. He placed his hands at the back of her head and began to gently thrust his hips. More and more of his length disappeared between her soft lips with each thrust. He didn't push her to take all of him down her throat. That would happen later when she was accustomed to his size.

One of her hands remained between his legs, caressing his tight balls. Her other hand moved around his hip and began fondling his ass, tickling along the separation of his cheeks. She felt his balls pull up tight against his body. She quickly inserted a finger into his anus while she continued to pump him with her mouth.

His sperm gushed out in spurts as orgasmic spasms pulsed through him. His chest rose and fell; his legs trembled. She gobbled up all of his hot cream, not missing a drop, then continued to suck on his undiminished prick.

Edward felt the power of his excitement surge through him. He knew the feeling well. This wasn't going to be a simple matter of some good sex—this was going to be hours of intense lovemaking. He wanted to experience everything she had learned. The matter of dealing with Jason would wait.

He opened the clasp on her bikini top and

released her breasts. They swung free, her hard nipples standing out erect and proud. He bent his head and took one of her nipples into his mouth, savoring the texture and taste. She was so exquisitely perfect, so divine. Without releasing her nipple from his mouth, he maneuvered her onto the bed.

He had missed the feel of her silky skin, the texture of her puckered nipples. He had been truly obsessed with her for a year, and now she was all his. He moved his mouth to her other nipple. His fingers untied the lacing of her bikini bottom and shoved the little bit of fabric aside. He tickled her inner thighs as she moved her hips against him.

How she had missed his sensual touch. Gunthar had been good, had made her scream with delight and experience delicious orgasms, but it was not the same type of intense ecstasy she experienced with Edward. Even the lightest touch of his fingertips set her body on fire.

Edward teased the underside of her breasts with his tongue and began kissing and tonguing his way down her body, finally arriving at her bush. He brushed the tip of his nose back and forth across her hard clit and inhaled her fragrance. His tongue traced along her pussy lips, already wet with excitement.

Rebecca shuddered when his warm breath tickled through her fur. She moaned, softly at first, then with increased elation when his tongue touched her pussy lips. Then, as if an uncontrollable force had been released, his mouth devoured her cunt. His tongue thrust into her wet opening, his lips closed around her clit. She screamed with euphoric delight as the first of many powerful orgasms ripped through her body. Her juices flooded his mouth, coating his cheeks and chin.

He couldn't get enough of her taste, or of the feel

of her pussy lips and clit. He drank in everything about her while she whimpered, writhed and ground her mount hard against his hungry mouth. She moved her hands to her breasts and pulled at her hard nipples. She didn't want this to end.

ELEVEN

Elsa and Gunthar viewed Jason with disgust as he cowered in the corner of the inner sanctum. He looked like a pathetic derelict. Gunthar spoke quietly to Elsa: "I think we should just hose him down and burn his clothes. I can't imagine Rebecca married to this scum."

He may have uttered the words quietly, but Rebecca's name carried to Jason's ears. His head jerked up and he snapped to attention. "What did you say? What was that about Rebecca?" There seemed to be a slight flicker of comprehension in his eyes, comprehension combined with a confused anxiousness.

Gunthar didn't acknowledge his question. "Take your clothes off, Jason. Pile them in the corner."

Jason mustered as much defiance and contempt as

he could. He sneered at Gunthar. "Fuck you, ass-hole."

Gunthar's face turned hard and a cold malevolence darted through his eyes. Jason flinched and took a quick step backward. Even though the two men were about the same height, Gunthar seemed to tower over Jason. With a movement so quick that Jason never saw it coming, Gunthar backhanded him across the side of the face and sent him sprawling across the floor.

Gunthar's voice was quiet and very commanding. "I expect to have my instructions followed to the letter without having to repeat them."

Jason's eyes never left Gunthar as he began to fumble with the buttons on his shirt. He soon stood in front of Gunthar and Elsa wearing only his briefs. Gunthar's words were harsh as he snapped them out. "Everything!"

Reluctantly, Jason removed his briefs and stood naked. Elsa was unable to contain herself. Her spontaneous laughter filled the room. "Look at him, darling. I've never seen such a little cock on a grown man." She slowly circled Jason. "Beer paunch and flabby butt—been spending too much time sitting on bar stools. Pasty white skin, lousy muscle tone."

When she completed her circuit, she reached out and tweaked his flaccid penis. "I really can't believe this little thing. How big does it get when it's hard? You don't need to answer that, we'll find out soon enough." With that, she turned and walked away, still laughing.

Gunthar motioned Jason across the room to a bathroom. "I want you to take three showers, and make sure you scrub every inch of your body."

Rebecca straddled Edward's hips as he lowered her

onto his hard cock. She had never felt anything like his magnificent organ penetrating to the farthest reaches of her love tunnel. He filled her like no one ever had. She felt her muscles grab his shaft, felt his cock twitch inside her box. Waves of rapture crashed through her body as she rocked back and forth on his rigid pole.

Her face reflected the passion that coursed through her veins. Her pussy walls closed tightly around his hard cock, squeezing his shaft with each wave of ecstasy that swept through her.

Edward's voice was husky and thick, his breathing ragged. "That's the hottest, wettest, tightest pussy I've ever had the pleasure of experiencing. You've learned your lessons well."

He pulled her face down and plastered his mouth to hers, thrusting past her lips with his demanding tongue. He wanted more and more of her. His hands slid across her bottom, kneading the firm curve of her cheeks. He slowly slipped his finger up her anus and heard her whimper with delight. Her pussy muscles worked his cock as she rocked hard against him, her clit rubbing against his pubic growth. He felt his control slipping away, his balls tightening against his body.

Time had no meaning as they continued their intense lovemaking. Her body was everything he wanted, everything he craved. She eagerly responded to any and all instructions with enthusiasm and a surprising amount of skill considering how new all of this was to her. She seemed to be able to instinctively anticipate his wants and needs. She knew which rhythm would best suit him, how and where to touch him, what excited him most.

The fires of passion burned in her eyes. She was lost in the throes of wanton lust, her total abandonment of conscious will.

He raised her by the hips and let his cock slide free as he turned her around. Then he pressed the head of his throbbing tool against her lubricated asshole. Without hesitation, Rebecca shoved her gorgeous ass back against him. Edward slowly penetrated her anus as he reached around her and fingered her clit. Her body immediately convulsed into yet another orgasm. She was so incredibly hot, so open to him. He didn't have to do any of the work. Rebecca took the initiative, riding his cock that was lodged so firmly up her ass. He simply leaned back and allowed her to set a rhythm that was comfortable for her. He was surprised when she began wiggling her ass at the same time as she pushed against him. She sought every avenue of pleasure. She had truly become more than he ever could have expected. He closed his eyes as Rebecca increased the tempo, her breathing ragged and her chest heaving. His own control was in doubt from her ministrations. Her ass was so tight; it felt as though she would wring every last drop of moisture from him. As the throes of her own orgasm overtook her, he could feel his sperm rise. As Rebecca settled against him one last time, he erupted into her dark channel, filling her ass with his cream.

Rebecca and Edward lay in bed, his arms wrapped around her body and his hands gently cupping her breasts. They were quietly enjoying the afterglow of intense lovemaking. For several hours they had engaged in every form of sex that two people can share.

"That was perfection, Rebecca. I am very pleased and," he brushed his lips across the nape of her neck and squeezed her firm breasts, "fully satisfied."

She snuggled next to his warm body, his words of praise igniting a glowing flame inside her. "Oh, Edward, that was so wonderful, I don't ever want it to end."

She turned her face toward him. He could see the excitement burning in her eyes. "So, my love goddess has developed an insatiable appetite while I was away." He lowered his mouth to hers, caressing it with a tender kiss. He turned her around until her love nest brushed against his mouth. He wanted more of her sweet taste.

Following lunch, Edward and Gunthar headed for the tennis court. Elsa and Rebecca lingered on the patio, preferring to watch them play from the comfort of the shaded table. There was also another reason why Elsa had suggested they remain behind. She was to try to obtain an insight into how badly Rebecca wanted revenge against Jason. Did she want it enough to give her approval to what was going to happen to him anyway, with or without her knowledge?

Elsa wasted no time in beating around the bush. Rebecca had become accustomed to her directness and had learned to respond in kind. "What would you do if I told you that Jason is here, on the island, and at our complete mercy? Would you want to see him punished for what he did to you—see him humiliated and victimized? Would you want him to know that you're here and fully approve of the proceedings?"

A look of confusion crossed Rebecca's face. "Jason? Here? How? Why? I don't understand." She searched Elsa's face for an explanation.

"How and why isn't important right now. The question is whether or not you would want to see him punished. How do you stand on that?" Elsa watched as Rebecca turned this surprise over in her mind.

At first Rebecca's voice was hesitant. "I'm not sure. I've thought about it many times over the years, especially the early years right after it happened." Her eyes took on an excited glow. She stared at Elsa for a long minute. "Yes! Yes, I'd like to see it. Not only would I like to actually witness it, I'd want him to know exactly why it was happening. I'd like it to happen to him just like it happened to me."

Elsa smiled and patted Rebecca's hand. "And so it shall." She turned her attention to the tennis game.

Later everyone changed into their bathing suits. For the first time Rebecca saw the marks on Elsa's back and legs. Time had helped to heal them; they didn't look as ugly and vicious as when they were fresh. Rebecca averted her eyes, not able to look at them. Noting Rebecca's response, Edward had a quick heated discussion with Gunthar about his having indulged his dark moods while involved with an assignment. After that the matter was forgotten.

The balance of the afternoon was spent playing in the pool. It was a free, easy and open time of fun and laughs. Everything was so relaxed. Rebecca couldn't remember the last time she had experienced this kind of innocent play. It was like being a child again.

Late that afternoon Gunthar and Edward had a private conversation at the side of the pool, then Gunthar and Elsa left. Edward made his way through the water to where Rebecca lay floating on a rubber raft. He grabbed the edge of the raft and pulled it slowly toward him until she was at his side. Without saying a word, he untied the laces on her bikini bottom and unclasped the bikini top. He tossed the two bits of fabric onto the deck surrounding the pool.

Edward skimmed his hands across her skin until he had touched her everywhere. Her nipples stood erect as her breasts rose and fell. Edward's own breathing wasn't as controlled as he would have liked. He slipped his hands underneath her bottom and lifted her pelvis out of the water. She immediately put her legs across his shoulders and around his neck. He leaned forward and placed a soft kiss on her pussy lips.

His voice was soft and teasing, his smile mischievous. "Tell me, my sexy beauty, have you ever been fucked into ecstasy in a swimming pool?"

Her look was sultry, her smile dazzling. She arched her hips toward him. "Not until now." She feigned a look of innocence. "That *is* what you're going to do, isn't it?"

His eyes turned a burning charcoal. "There's not a force on earth that can stop me."

Edward smiled. She was his in every way, especially now that she had expressed desire for revenge against Jason. He already owned her body. Now he had drawn up the unwritten contract for her soul...and she was about to sign it. After this night, the transaction would be complete. He smiled inwardly as he pushed her against the side of the pool, raised her hips and floated her toward his upstanding prick. He penetrated her slowly as he held her by the breasts.

It was dark when Edward escorted Rebecca into the entertainment room and turned on the television. Gunthar and Elsa were not with them. He sat on the floor, his back resting against the couch, and positioned her on the floor between his spread legs. She snuggled back against his body, held protectively in his embrace. He felt her body stiffen when she saw Jason's face appear on the screen.

Rebecca's heart pounded and her body shivered as she watched the scene unfolding in front of her eyes. She didn't know what to think or what to feel; it was all so totally unexpected.

She watched, mesmerized, as an amazonian woman dressed only in a black garter belt, net stockings and spike heels, stepped off a platform in the middle of a bare room and walked toward Jason. He had been stripped of all his clothes and had been strapped across some kind of hitching post. A little flicker of pleasure danced inside her when she saw how frightened Jason looked.

Monica stood in front of Jason's face and thrust her pussy toward his mouth. Her voice was hard and cold. "Eat my cunt! Make me scream for mercy!" Without further conversation she pressed her crotch against his mouth.

Nothing happened. Jason made no attempt to comply with her orders. She continued to press her cunt against his mouth.

Her words became menacing. "You little bastard. Either do as you're told, and you better do a good job of it, or I'll take my whip and turn your butt into hamburger." She thrust her hips again, shoving her pussy hard against his mouth.

Jason looked up at Monica looming over him. He knew that she meant what she said. He stuck out his tongue and lapped at her pussy lips.

Monica remained impassive as if bored by the entire proceeding. She registered no excitement of any kind, no signs of arousal. No matter how hard Jason tried, no matter what he did, Monica remained unmoved. His tongue flicked, licked, lapped—his mouth sucked on her clit and tugged at her pussy lips. She remained unmoved. She stood with her pussy pressed to his mouth for half an hour.

"I've never encountered anyone as lousy as you are—you don't know the first thing about eating pussy. And this," she reached between his legs and tugged at his limp cock, "is an even more pathetic thing. You must be the laughingstock of every woman in Boston." She released his tool and took a step back from him.

Jason was clearly humiliated. He closed his eyes, unable to meet her look of total and complete contempt. He didn't understand why this was happening to him or who these people were.

"You're obviously no good with women. Perhaps it's because you really prefer men." A glow of cruel delight danced in her eyes as she suggested the next activity on the agenda.

Jason's head jerked up and his eyes snapped open at the sound of Monica's words. Panic crossed his face as a burly man stepped around in front of him.

Topu took up his position in front of Jason's face and planted his large feet solidly on the floor. His grin showed three missing teeth. His huge, hairy balls hung heavy beneath his enormous, throbbing cock. He reached for Jason's limp prick. His grin widened and turned into a laugh. "Look! He has a little boy dick. Topu's dick was bigger than that when he was ten years old." He wiggled Jason's small organ back and forth and continued to laugh.

The laughter stopped; the grin left Topu's face. He wrapped his hand around his own shaft and touched the swollen head to Jason's lips. Jason recoiled, turning his head away. Topu grabbed Jason's hair and yanked his head back. Again, he touched the darkening helmet to Jason's lips.

Monica's voice was curt. "Take it in your mouth. You can't eat pussy worth shit, let's see how you are at sucking cock. There must be something you know how to do." She cracked the whip she was holding, the sound adding emphasis to her words.

Rebecca watched the television screen, repulsed and fascinated at the same time. Slowly the fascination won out and she stared intently. She felt Edward's arms tighten around her, and he kissed her softly on the nape of the neck. She placed her hands of top of his, absorbing his warmth and strength. She continued to watch the screen.

Monica circled around behind Jason. He was clearly nervous and tried to turn his head to see what she was doing. Topu jerked Jason's head forward so that he couldn't see Monica. He put his cock to Jason's mouth again. "You better take it or she'll punish you for sure." Topu grinned again. "She loves to give punishment." No sooner were the words out of Topu's mouth than Jason felt the sting of the leather strap across his bare ass.

Jason opened his mouth to groan and Topu inserted his hard rod. Jason closed his eyes and began to suck as best he could. Less than five minutes later Topu pulled his cock out of Jason's mouth and turned toward Monica. "He can't suck cock either." He turned back toward Jason. "You're pretty worthless. What good are you?"

A hard, cruel smile turned the corners of Monica's mouth. Still behind Jason where he couldn't see her, she reached her hands to his ass and grabbed both cheeks. Her words cut through the air like a sharp knife. "Maybe he's got a real hot ass."

A bolt of fear shot through Jason as he saw the grin spread across Topu's face and felt Monica's hands spread his buttocks apart. His throat went dry, his stomach churned. He knew what was about to happen, and he also knew there was absolutely nothing he could do to prevent it. Topu disappeared from his line of sight. He felt Monica's hands being replaced by Topu's rough meathooks. He closed his eyes and tried to brace himself against the buttfucking that was coming.

Edward kissed Rebecca's neck and cupped her breasts in his warm hands. He whispered in her ear, "I can stop this right now if you want me to," he kissed her on the cheek, "or you can get your final revenge. The decision is yours. Which will it be, Rebecca?"

She turned and looked up at Edward. Her eyes widened in surprise. "You mean this is happening right now? This isn't a tape?"

"That's right. This is a live picture, not a recording." He waited for her response.

She knew it was wrong; revenge wouldn't change what had already happened. She knew decency dictated that she tell Edward to stop what was going on. However, none of that mattered—she wanted Jason to suffer. Her words were emphatic. "Do it!"

Edward smiled and brushed his lips against hers. It was done. She had just signed the contract. He now possessed her soul as well as her body.

Topu touched the tip of his cock to Jason's anus. Then, without warning, he buried it all the way up his ass. Jason screamed—a tight, choking scream, as though he were having to force it past his throat—and then let go and simply howled. Topu didn't pause, didn't allow Jason to catch his breath or to assimilate what was happening. Topu simply

207

rammed his stiff rod in and out with vigorous, harsh strokes. He seemed to be deaf to Jason's screams. He slammed against Jason's buttocks, using the entire length of his huge shaft. He kept pumping until his body stiffened and his hot cream filled Jason's ass.

Topu withdrew his organ. He grabbed Jason's buttocks in his hands and gave them a rough squeeze. "Finally found something this guy can do," he laughed.

Monica moved in front of Jason. His face was still contorted from the pain and his chest heaved. She reached between his legs and grabbed his stiffening cock. "Well, well, well...it seems you're finally able to get it up. I guess we did find something you like." She sneered and let out a cruel laugh. "Not that it really matters, though. This pathetic little thing couldn't satisfy anyone."

Monica again circled behind him to give him one final kiss of the whip across his ass. Topu's semen, tinged with blood, oozed from Jason's asshole and dribbled down his leg. Her final words caused a chill of fear to settle inside him. "Since you seem to enjoy this more than anything else, Topu will come back later to give you a second helping."

Monica moved around him until her crotch was positioned in front of his face. She thrust her hips forward and rubbed her muff against his nose. Her voice was cold and harsh. "Rebecca sends her regards. She hopes you're deriving as much pleasure from this as she did from your tender care on her honeymoon."

Edward picked up the remote and clicked off the television. He turned Rebecca around until she faced him. "Well? Was it everything you hoped it would be?"

Her eyes glowed with excitement. "I'm ashamed

at how good it made me feel, especially having him know it was me. I'm ashamed...but I loved it."

He stroked her long hair and cupped her chin with his hand. Edward smiled, a disturbingly sinister smile, and his eyes burned with an odd light. "Revenge is sweet. It heightens the senses, makes the blood race through the veins, makes the entire being come alive. Welcome into the fold. There will be many more delights for you."

Rebecca felt an inexplicable wariness surge through her body—something about the expression on Edward's face combined with the words he had spoken. She didn't know what to make of it, but it made her feel slightly uneasy. Any further thoughts on the subject were immediately dismissed, however, as he captured her mouth with a delicious kiss.

Elsa and Gunthar soon reappeared, and dinner was served on the patio. The conversation was light with no mention of Jason, as if the incident had never happened. When the last of the dinner dishes had been cleared away, the four of them adjourned to Rebecca's suite.

Elsa and Gunthar immediately fell into the bed, and he buried his mouth in her abundant pussy fur. Rebecca and Edward joined them and soon there was a tangled pile of bodies in the middle of the bed—arms, legs, mouths, cocks and cunts all greedily merging into a single heaving mass.

Several hours later everyone's attention was again turned to Jason. Edward clicked on the television in the entertainment room and situated Rebecca between his legs as before. He felt her breathing quicken as the picture appeared before her.

Topu stood in front of Jason and tugged on Jason's limp cock. A grin spread across the big islander's face. "Little boy dick, how funny." Then Topu moved behind him.

Topu's large hands grabbed Jason's ass and spread his cheeks apart. Without a word or a moment's hesitation he rammed his rigid prick all the way into Jason's battered and swollen anus. Jason screamed and screamed as the pain seared through him. Topu laughed and pumped him with hard strokes.

It was late. The villa had become very quiet. Jason had been released from his bindings, put on the jet and returned to Boston. Gunthar had carefully explained to him how useless it would be for him to report the incident to the police. He couldn't identify his abductors, he didn't know where he had been taken, he couldn't prove a connection between himself and someone of Edward's stature. He couldn't even provide a motive. Edward could produce a dozen reputable witnesses who would swear he was in Boston the entire time Jason would claim to have been on the island with him. Gunthar also warned him of the dire consequences of attempting any type of retaliation.

Rebecca was tired. It had been a long day filled with the delicious, long awaited taste of revenge. It had also ended with a disturbing feeling that she couldn't identify, something about the way Edward had looked at her and the words he had spoken.

Edward took Rebecca's hand and led her to his bedroom. "Your things have been moved. You will sleep with me in my room from now on. The suite will be used for other guests. We will be returning to Boston in three days. A business associate of mine will be arriving first thing in the morning to enjoy the hospitality of the island." He removed her clothes, then his own.

He laid her on his bed and stretched out next to her. His fingers tickled across her pussy fur as his tongue teased her nipples to taut peaks. "You will be entertaining him." He felt her body stiffen as he slipped a finger between her delicate pussy lips. She started to say something, but he continued talking before she could get any words out.

"He likes being spanked, paddled actually, until his bottom is bright red. This gives him a raging hard-on. After you've paddled his ass until it glows in the dark, he'll sit down on a hard wooden chair—this causes him a great deal of discomfort without being too painful. He'll want you to stand very close to him so that your pussy is almost in his face and slowly finger-fuck yourself."

Edward slipped a second finger inside Rebecca's love nest and brushed her clit with his thumb. "He'll watch you, never touching you, until he shoots all over himself. The whole thing usually takes less than ten minutes."

Rebecca shivered as she listened to his words. So this was how it was going to be. She had made her deal. She had sold her soul to the devil and now he was going to collect his due.

A delicious rush of ecstasy shot through her body as Edward buried his mouth in her pussy. His tongue flicked in and out of her wet opening, then his lips closed over her engorged clit. *If this is hell, then I'll gladly suffer it*. It was her last conscious thought before thrusting her crotch hard against his mouth. Rebecca whimpered and screamed as she exploded into a series of intense orgasms.

Other Books Available From
MASQUERADE'S
EROTIC LIBRARY

PAUL LITTLE

SLAVE ISLAND   **3006-7**   **$4.95**

The passenger ship *Anastasia* is lured to an uncharted island in the Pacific. Those on board soon learn this is no ordinary paradise. For Lord Henry Philbrock, a sadistic genius, has built a hidden compound where captives are forced into slavery. They are trained to accommodate the most bizarre sexual cravings of the rich, the famous, the pampered and the perverted. Beyond all civilized boundaries!

THE AUTOBIOGRAPHY OF A FLEA III   **94-7**   **$4.95**

That incorrigible voyeur, the Flea, returns for yet another tale of outrageous acts and indecent behavior. This time Flea returns to Provence to spy on the younger generation, now just coming into their own ripe, juicy maturity. With the same wry wit and eye for lurid detail, the Flea's secret observations won't fail to titillate yet again!

END OF INNOCENCE   **77-7**   **$4.95**

The early days of Women's Emancipation are the setting for this story of some very independent ladies. These girls were willing to go to any lengths to fight for their sexual freedom, and willing to endure any punishment in their desire for total liberation. You've come a long way, baby!

CELESTE   **75-0**   **$4.95**

It's definitely all in the family for this female duo of sexual dynamos. While traveling through Europe, these two try everything and everyone on their horny holiday. Neither is afraid of trying anything new or different, including each other!

RED DOG SALOON   **68-8**   **$4.95**

Quantrill's Raiders pillaged Kansas during the Civil War. Bella Denburg took a vow to avenge one of their victims, her cousin Genevieve, who was kidnapped and raped. Bella intended to get herself accepted as a camp follower of Quantrill, find the men responsible, and kill them. Her pursuit led her through whorehouses, rapes, and tar-and-featherings until at last, unsuspecting, she held each of the guilty ones between her legs. Lust and revenge!

CHINESE JUSTICE AND OTHER STORIES   **57-2**   **$4.95**

On the Eve of the Boxer Rebellion in China, Li Woo, the Magistrate of Hanchow, swore to destroy all foreign devils. Then he would subject their women to sexual sports, hanging them upside down from pulleys while his two lesbian torturers applied whips to their tender, naked flesh. Afterwards, he would force them to perform fellatio on his guests as his torturers whipped them. This lay in store for every foreign woman in Hanchow!

THE EDITORS OF PLAYGIRL

PLAYGIRL FANTASIES   13-0 $4.95

Here are the best and hottest female fantasies from the "Readers' Fantasy Forum" of *Playgirl*, the erotic magazine for women. From a passenger who pays her fare in the back seat of a cab, to a sexy surveyor who likes to give construction workers the lay of the land, to a female choreographer who enjoys creating X-rated dances with a variety of perverted partners, these 38 fantasies will drive you wild.

MORE PLAYGIRL FANTASIES   69-6 $4.95

The editors of *Playgirl* bring you more of their favorites from the "Readers' Fantasy Forum." This collection is even hotter than the last, as the readers of *Playgirl* share their most intimate and imaginative fantasy encounters, revealing every steamy detail—daydreams only *Playgirl* readers could pen!

THE MASQUERADE READERS

DOUBLE NOVEL   86-6 $6.95

Two bestselling novels of illicit desire, combined into one spellbinding volume! Paul Little's *The Metamorphosis of Lisette Joyaux* tells the story of an innocent young woman seduced by a group of beautiful and experienced lesbians who initiate her into a new world of pleasure. *The Story of Monique* explores an underground society's clandestine rituals and scandalous encounters that beckon to the ripe and willing Monique.

A MASQUERADE READER   84-X $4.95

Masquerade presents a salacious selection of excerpts from its library of erotica. Infamously strict lessons are learned at the hand of *The English Governess* and *Nina Foxton*, where the notorious Nina proves herself a very harsh taskmistress. Scandalous confessions are to be found in the *Diary of an Angel*, and the harrowing story of a woman whose desires drove her to the ultimate sacrifice in *Thongs* completes this collection. Leaves you hungry for more!

EASTERN EROTICA

KAMA HOURI   39-4 $4.95

Ann Pemberton, daughter of the British regimental commander in India, runs away with her servant. Forced to live in a harem, Ann accepts her sexual submission and offers herself to any warrior who wishes to mount her. The natives kindle a fire within her and Ann, sexually ablaze, became a legend as the white sex-bitch of Indian legend!

ROBERT DESMOND

PROFESSIONAL CHARMER   3003-2 $4.95

A dissolute gigolo lives a parasitical life of luxury by providing his sexual services to the rich and bored. Traveling in the most exclusive social circles, this gun-for-hire will gratify the lewdest and most vulgar cravings for nothing more than a fine meal or a shred of stylish clothing. Each and every exploit he must perform is described in lurid detail, in this story of a prostitute's progress!

THE SWEETEST FRUIT 95-5 $4.95

A twisted tale of revenge and seduction! Connie Lashfield is determined to seduce and destroy pious Father Chadcroft to show her former lover, Ben Trawler, that she no longer requires his sexual services. She corrupts the priest into forsaking all that he holds sacred, destroys his peaceful parish, and slyly manipulates him with her smouldering looks and hypnotic sexual aura. But little does she know that he's followed her lecherous lead—and taken a saucy lover of his own!

PETER JASON

WAYWARD 3004-0 $4.95

A mysterious countess hires a bus and tour guide for an unusual vacation. Traveling through Europe's most notorious cities and resorts, the bus picks up the countess' friends, lovers, and acquaintances from every walk of life. The common thread between these strangers is their libertine philosophy and pursuit of unbridled sensual pleasure. Each guest brings unique sexual tastes and talents to the group, climaxing in countless orgies, outrageous acts, and endless deviation!

THE CLASSIC COLLECTION

THE YELLOW ROOM 96-3 $4.95

Two complete erotic masterpieces. The "yellow room" holds the secrets of lust, lechery and the lash. There, bare-bottomed, spread-eagled and open to the world, demure Alice Darvell soon learns to love her lickings from her perverted guardian. Even more exciting is the second torrid tale of hot heiress Rosa Coote and her adventures in punishment and pleasure with her two sexy, sadistic servants, Jane and Jemima. Feverishly erotic!

THE BOUDOIR 85-8 $4.95

Masquerade presents a new edition of the classic Victorian magazine, including several bawdy novellas, ribald stories, and indecent anecdotes to arouse and delight. Six volumes of this original journal of indiscretion are presented here in all their salacious glory. Good old-fashioned smut!

A WEEKEND VISIT 59-9 $4.95

"Dear Jack, Can you come down for a long weekend visit and amuse three lonely females? I am writing at mother's suggestion. Do come!" Fresh from his erotic exploits in *Man with a Maid*, randy Jack is at it again!

TICKLED PINK 58-0 $4.95

From her spyroom, Emily sees her aunt, Lady Lovesport, lash her maid into a frenzy, and then tongue-whip her as Mr. Everard enters the bounteous Lovesport's behind. Emily is joined in her spying by young Harry, who practices the positions he observes. An erotic vacation!

THE ENGLISH GOVERNESS 43-2 $4.95

When Lord Lovell's son was expelled from his prep school for masturbation, his father hired a governess to tutor the motherless boy—giving her strict instructions not to spare the rod to break him of his bad habits. But governess Harriet Marwood was addicted to domination. The whip was her loving instrument. With it, she taught young Richard Lovell to use the rod in ways he had never dreamed possible. The downward path to perversion!

SACRED PASSIONS   21-1 $4.95
Young Augustus comes into the heavenly sanctuary, seeking protection from the enemies of his debt-ridden father. Soon he discovers that the joys of the body far surpass those of the spirit.

THE NUNNERY TALES   20-3 $4.95
Innocent novices are helpless in the hands of corrupt clerics. The Abbess forces her rites of sexual initiation on any maiden who falls into her hands. Father Abelard delivers his penance with smart strokes of the whip on his female penitents' bottoms. After exposure to the Mother Superior and her lustful nuns, sweet Emilie, Louise, and the other novices are sexual novices no longer. Cloistered concubinage!

MAN WITH A MAID   15-7 $4.95
The ultimate epic of sexual domination. In the "Snuggery," a padded, sound-proofed room equipped with wall pulleys, a strap-down table, and a chair with hand and leg shackles, untiring pervert Jack bends beautiful Alice to his will. She not only gives in to his lewd desire, she becomes more lascivious than he. She corrupts her maid and her best friend into lesbianism. Then the three girls lure a voluptuous mother and her demure daughter into the Snuggery for a forcible seduction and orgy. Perhaps the all-time hottest book!

FRUITS OF PASSION   05-X $4.95
A classic study of Victorian sexual obsession. From his initiation into endless orgiastic delights by the slippery lips of the chambermaid sisters, Rose and Manette, the Count de Leon continues his erotic diary for forty years, ending with his Caribbean voyages with the two most uninhibited Victorian Venuses he has ever known. A life totally dedicated to sex!

ALEXANDER TROCCHI

WHITE THIGHS   3009-1 $4.95
A dark fantasy of sexual obsession from a modern erotic master, Alexander Trocchi. This is the story of young Saul and his sexual fixation on beautiful, tormented Anna of the white thighs. Their scorching, dangerous passion leads to murder and madness every time they submit. Saul must possess her again and again, no matter what or who stands in his way. A powerful and disturbing masterpiece!

SCHOOL FOR SIN   89-0 $4.95
When Peggy Flynn leaves the harsh morality of her Irish country home behind for the bright lights of Dublin, her sensuous nature leads to her seduction by a handsome and mysterious stranger. He recruits her into a training school with an uncommon curriculum. Together with the other students, she embarks on an unusual education in erotic pleasures. No one knows what awaits them at graduation, but each student is sure to be well-schooled in sex!

YOUNG ADAM   63-7 $4.95
Two British barge operators discover a girl drowned in the river Clyde. Her lover, a plumber, is arrested for her murder. But he is innocent. Joe, the barge assistant, knows that. As the plumber is tried and sentenced to hang, this knowledge lends poignancy to Joe's romances with the women along the river whom he will love then...well, read on.

MY LIFE AND LOVES (THE 'LOST' VOLUME) 52-1 $4.95
What happens when you try to fake a sequel to the most scandalous autobiography of the 20th century? If the "forger" is one of the most important figures in modern Erotica, you get a masterpiece, and *this is it!*

THONGS $4.95

"Spain, perhaps more than any other country in the world, is the land of passion and of death. And in Spain life is cheap, from that glittering tragedy in the bullring to the quick thrust of the stiletto in a narrow street in a Barcelona slum. No, this death would not have called for further comment had it not been for one striking fact. The naked woman had met her end in a way he had never seen before—a way that had enormous sexual significance. My God, she had been..."

THE CARNAL DAYS OF HELEN SEFERIS 35-1 $4.95

Private Investigator Anthony Harvest takes on his greatest challenge. He is determined to find and save Helen Seferis, a beautiful Australian who has been abducted in Algiers. Following clues in Helen's diary, he flies to North Africa and descends into the depths of the white-slave trade. Through exotic slave markets, forbidden harems, and sadistic rites he pursues Helen Seferis, the ultimate sexual prize!

CLASSIC EROTIC BIOGRAPHIES

THE STORY OF MONIQUE 42-4 $4.95

Lovely, innocent Monique found her aunt's friends strange, curious, inviting. There were seven lesbians who came to Aunt Sonia's parties. And a convent nearby where nuns and monks whipped themselves into a frenzy and then fell upon each other in orgiastic madness. Monique became the mistress of *all* their ceremonies; and discovered within herself an endless appetite for sex—the more perverted, the better.!

THE MISFORTUNES OF MARY 27-0 $4.95

Mary came from her uncle's parsonage in Ireland to be a writer's assistant in London, in response to an ad run in the *Gazette* by Mrs. Coates. But the lady was a procuress, and the writer was a libertine who paid a hundred pounds for Mary's virginity. As he broke her in, Mrs. Coates sold spectator seats in her secret viewing room to Lord Strongcock and his randy friends. Then she sold the no-longer-virginal Mary to them. White-hot white slavery!

THE FURTHER ADV. OF MADELEINE 04-1 $4.95

"What mortal pen can describe these driven orgasmic transports," writes Madeleine as she explores Paris' sexual underground. She discovers that the finest clothes may cover the most twisted personalities of all—especially the that of mad monk Grigory Rasputin, whose sexual drives match even Madeleine's. History-making sex!

THE MASQUERADE AMERICAN COLLECTION

DANCE HALL GIRLS 44-0 $4.95

The dance hall studio in Modesto was a ruthless trap for women of all ages. They learned to dance under the tutelage of sexual professionals. So grateful were they for the attention, they opened their hearts and their wallets. Scandalous sexual slavery!

LUSTY LESSONS 31-9 $4.95

David Elston had everything; good breeding, money, a secure job with a promising future, and a beautiful wife—everything except the ability to fulfill the unrelenting demands of his passion. His efforts to satisfy his desires end in failure...until he meets a voluptuous stranger who takes him in hand and leads him to the forbidden land of unattainable pleasure.

THE GILDED LILY 25-4 $4.95

Lily Caldron, struggling actress, knows what she wants—pleasure, passion, and new experiences. But more than that, she wants her big break—one that will launch her career in the movies. She looks for it at Hollywood's most private party, where nothing is forbidden and the only rule is sexual excess. There she meets one of Tinseltown's hottest directors, and becomes submerged in a world of secrets and perversions she never imagined.

JOCELYN JOYCE

THE WILD HEART 007-5 $4.95

A luxurious hotel in Switzerland in the setting for this artful web of sex, desire, and love. A newlywed wife sees sex as a conjugal duty, while her hungry husband tries to awaken her. An opportunistic hotel employee entertains the wealthy guests on the side for money. A swinging couple introduce some new ideas into the marriage of two American guests. A delicious variation on the old Inn-and-out!

PRIVATE LIVES 91-2 $4.95

The wealthy French suburb of Dampierre is the setting for this racy soap opera of non-stop action! The illicit affairs and lecherous habits of Dampierre's most illustrious citizens make for a sizzling tale of French erotic life. The wealthy widow who has a craving for a young busboy, who is sleeping with a rich businessman's wife, whose husband is minding his sex business elsewhere, are just a few of Dampierre's randy residents. An unrestrained look at the more sophisticated side of French life!

DEMON HEAT 79-3 $4.95

An ancient vampire stalks the unsuspecting in the form of a beautiful woman. Unlike the legendary Dracula, this fiend doesn't drink blood; she craves a different kind of potion. When her insatiable appetite has drained every last drop of juice from her victims, she leaves them spent and hungering for more—even if it means being sucked to death!

HAREM SONG 73-4 $4.95

Young Amber flees her cruel uncle and provincial English village in search of a better life, but finds she is no match for the streets of London. Amber becomes a classy call girl and is eventually sold into a lusty Sultan's harem—a vocation for which she possesses more than average talent!

JADE EAST 60-2 $4.95

Laura, passive and passionate, follows her domineering husband Emilio to Hong Kong. He gives her to Wu Li, a Chinese connoisseur of sexual perversions, who passes her on to Madeleine, a flamboyant lesbian. Madeleine's friends make Laura the centerpiece in Hong Kong's underground orgies. As she is being taken by three men while the guests watch, Laura sees Emilio with a beautiful, dark-haired girl: he is about to start another on her downward path. A journey into sexual slavery!

RAWHIDE LUST 55-6 $4.95

Diana Beaumont, the young wife of a U.S. Marshal, is kidnapped as an act of vengeance against her husband. Jack Beaumont sets out on a long journey to get his wife back, but finally catches up with her trail only to learn that she's been sold into Mexico. A story of the Old West, when the only law was made by the gun, and a woman's virtue was often worth no more than the price of a few steers!

THE JAZZ AGE   48-3 $4.95

This is an erotic novel of life in the Roaring Twenties. A Wall Street attorney becomes suspicious of his mistress while his wife has an interlude with a lesbian lover. *The Jazz Age* is a romp of erotic realism in the heyday of the flapper and the speakeasy.

LUSCIDIA WALLACE

THE ICE MAIDEN   3001-6 $4.95

Edward Canton has ruthlessly seized everything he wants in life, with one exception: Rebecca Esterbrook. Frustrated by his inability to seduce her with money, he kidnaps her and whisks her away to his remote island compound, where she learns to shed her inhibitions and accept caresses from both men and women. Fully aroused for the first time in her life, she becomes his writhing, red-hot love slave!

KATY'S AWAKENING   74-2 $4.95

Poor Katy thinks she's been rescued by a kindly young couple after a terrible car wreck. Little does she suspect that she's been ensnared by a ring of swingers whose tastes run to domination and wild sex parties. Katy becomes the newest initiate into this private club, and learns the rules from every player!

ALIZARIN LAKE

THE INSTRUMENTS OF THE PASSION   3010-5 $4.95

All that remains is the diary of a young initiate, detailing the twisted rituals of a mysterious cult institution known only as "Russiter". Behind these sinister walls, a beautiful young woman performs an unending drama of pain and humiliation. What is the impulse that justifies her, night after night, to consent to this strange ceremony? And to what lengths will her aberrant passion drive her?

CLARA   80-7 $4.95

The mysterious death of a beautiful, aristocratic woman leads her old boyfriend on a harrowing journey of discovery. His search uncovers a woman on a quest for deeper and more unusual sensations, each more shocking than the one before!

TUTORED IN LUST   78-5 $4.95

This tale of the initiation and instruction of a carnal college co-ed and her fellow students unlocks the sex secrets of the classroom. Books take a back seat to secret societies and their bizarre ceremonies, in this story of students with an unquenchable thirst for knowledge!

DIARY OF AN ANGEL   71-8 $4.95

A long-forgotten diary tells the story of angelic Victoria, lured into a secret life of unimaginable depravity. "I am like a fly caught in a spider's web, a helpless and voiceless victim of their every whim." This intelligent and shocking novel is destined to become an underground classic.

BUSINESS AS USUAL   56-4 $4.95

Alain, president of a Parisian import firm, awoke to find his maid beneath his covers while his wife bathed in the next room. On his arrival at work, Alain took the youngest of his three secretaries on his couch in his office, while his other two secretaries listened to her moans on the intercom and pleasured each other A customer arrived to relieve their frustations in a threesome. And this was just the warm-up for the afternoon and evening's sexual entertainment which Alain and the customer had planned. Non-stop sexual business!

FESTIVAL OF VENUS   37-8 $4.95

Brigeen Mooney fled her home in the west of Ireland to avoid being forced into a nunnery. But her refuge in Dublin turned out to be dedicated to a different religion. The young women she met there belonged to the Old Religion, devoted to sex and sacrifices. They were competing to become sexual priestesses on the Isle of Man. The sexual ceremonies of pagan gods!

CHINA BLUE

SECRETS OF THE CITY   03-3 $4.75

Her beautiful daughters, fifteen-year-old Eurasian twins, have been abducted by Thai pirates and sold into white slavery. China Blue, the infamous Madame of Saigon, a black belt enchantress in the martial arts of love, is out for revenge. Her search brings her to Manhattan, where she intends to call upon her secret sexual arts to kill her enemies at the height of ecstasy. A sex war!

MARY LOVE

VICE PARK PLACE   3008-3 $4.95

Rich, lonely divorcée Penelope Luckner drinks alone every night, fending off the advances of sexual suitors that she secretly craves. Alone, she dreams of a lover who can melt her frigid façade. Then she meets Robbie, a much younger man with a virgin's aching appetites, and together they embark on an affair that breaks all their fantasies wide open!

MASTERING MARY SUE   3005-9 $4.95

Mary Sue is a rich nymphomaniac whose husband is determined to pervert her, declare her mentally incompetent, and gain control of her fortune. He brings her to a castle in Europe, where a sadistic psychiatrist and his well-trained manservant amuse themselves with disciples recruited from a local private school. To Mary Sue's delight, they have stumbled on an unimaginably depraved sex cult, where panting men and women suffer beneath cruel instructors and every kind of corruption is practiced!

WANDA   3002-4 $4.95

Wanda just can't help it. Ever since she moved to Greenwich Village, she's been overwhelmed by the desire to be totally, utterly naked! By day, she finds herself inspired by a pornographic novel whose main character's insatiable appetites seem to match her own. At night she parades her quivering, nubile flesh in a non-stop sex show for her neighbors. An electrifying exhibitionist gone wild!

ANGELA   76-9 $4.95

A lonely bartender in a Parisian café thinks he's run every con in the book, until a mysterious woman walks in from of the cold and changes his mind. Angela's game is "look but don't touch," and she drives everyone crazy with desire, dancing and writhing for their viewing pleasure but never allowing a single caress. Soon her sensual spell is cast, and she's the only one who can break it!

HARRIET DAIMLER

THE PLEASURE THIEVES   36-X $4.95

They come in the night, cleaning out the contents of the safe while the orgy rages downstairs. They are the Pleasure Thieves, Harry and Philip, a pair of ex-cellmates and lovers whose sexually preoccupied targets are set up by Carol Stoddard, the publisher of *Femme* magazine. She forms a sexual threesome with them, trying every combination from two-on-ones to daisy chains—because forbidden pleasure are even sweeter when they're stolen!

LOUISE BELHAVEL

FORBIDDEN DELIGHTS   81-5 $4.95
Clara and Iris make their sexual debut in this Chronicle of the Forbidden.
Sexual taboos are what turn this pair on, as they travel the globe in search of
the next erotic threshold. The effect they have on their fellow world travel-
ers is definitely contagious!

FRAGRANT ABUSES   88-2 $4.95
The sex saga of Clara and Iris continues as the now-experienced girls enjoy
themselves with a new circle of worldly friends whose imaginations definitely match their own. Against an exotic array of locations, Clara and Iris sample the unique delights of every country and its culture!

DEPRAVED ANGELS   92-0 $4.95
The third and final installment in the incredible adventures of Clara and
Iris. Together with their friends, lovers, and worldly acquaintances, Clara
and Iris explore the frontiers of depravity at home and abroad. Their scandalous sexcapades delight and intrigue everyone, and their natural curiosity
and sweet, sexy personalities guarantee that there will always be new and
exotic thrills for them to experience just over the next horizon!

TITIAN BERESFORD

JUDITH BOSTON   87-4 $4.95
Young Edward would have been lucky to get the stodgy old companion he
thought his parents had hired for him. Instead, an exquisite woman arrives at
his door, and from the top of her tightly-wound bun to the tips of her impos-
sibly high heels, Judith Boston is in complete control. Edward finds his com-
pulsively lewd behavior never goes unpunished by the unflinchingly severe
Judith Boston!

NINA FOXTON   71-8 $4.95
A young aristocrat finds herself bored by the run-of-the-mill amusements
for ladies of good breeding. Instead of taking tea with gentlemen, outrageous Nina invents a device to "milk" them of their most private essences.
No one says "No" to Nina!

SINCERITY JONES

SEDUCTIONS   83-1 $4.95
Twelve short stories of erotic encounters, told with a woman's sensibility.
This original collection includes couplings of every variety, including a
woman who helps fulfill her man's fantasy of making it with another man, a
dangerous liaison in the back of a taxi, a uncommon alliance between a Wall
Street type and a funky, downtown woman, and a walk on the wild side for a
vacationing sexual adventurer. Thoroughly modern women!

PALMIRO VICARION

LUST   82-3 $4.95
A wealthy and powerful man of leisure recounts his rise up the corporate
ladder and his corresponding descent into debauchery. Adventure and polit-
ical intrigue provide a stimulating backdrop for this tale of a classic
scoundrel with an uncurbed appetite for sexual power!

MARCUS VAN HELLER

ADAM & EVE   93-9 $4.95

A young couple, Adam and Eve, long to escape their dull lives by achieving
stardom—she in the theater, and he in the art scene. They're willing to do
anything to become successful, including trading their luscious bodies for a
big break. Eve soon finds herself acting cozy on the casting couch, while
Adam must join a bizarre sex cult to further his artistic career. Corruption is
the price paid for fame in this electrifying tale of ambition and desire!

KIDNAP   90-4 $4.95

Nick Harding is called in to investigate a mysterious kidnapping case involv-
ing the rich and powerful in London, France and Geneva. Along the way he
has the pleasure of "interrogating" a sensuous exotic dancer named Jeanne
and a beautiful English reporter, as he finds himself further enmeshed in the
sleazy international crime underworld. A sizzling mystery of sexual intrigue
and betrayal!

A Complete Listing Of
MASQUERADE'S
EROTIC LIBRARY

ORDERING IS EASY!

MC/VISA ORDERS CAN BE PLACED BY CALLING OUR TOLL-FREE NUMBER

1-800-458-9640

OR MAIL THE COUPON BELOW TO:
MASQUERADE BOOKS
801 SECOND AVE.,
NEW YORK, N.Y. 10017

IM 001-6

QTY	TITLE	NO.	PRICE
	SUBTOTAL		
	POSTAGE and HANDLING		
	TOTAL		

Add $1.00 Postage and Handling for first book and 50¢ for each additional book. Outside the U.S. add $2.00 for first book, $1.00 for each additional book. New York state residents add 8 ¼% sales tax.

NAME _____

ADDRESS _____ APT # _____

CITY_____ STATE _____ ZIP _____

TEL ( ) _____

PAYMENT: ☐ CHECK   ☐ MONEY ORDER   ☐ VISA   ☐ MC

CARD NO. _____ EXP. DATE _____

PLEASE ALLOW **4-6 WEEKS** DELIVERY. NO C.O.D. ORDERS. PLEASE MAKE ALL CHECKS PAYABLE TO MASQUERADE BOOKS. PAYABLE IN U.S. CURRENCY ONLY.